Harry Hop-Pole

Wispy Gorman

This edition published in Great Britain by

acorn book company

www.acornbook.co.uk

ISBN 978-0-9568628-0-8

British Library Cataloguing in Publication Data.
A catalogue record for this book is available from the British Library.

First published in 2011.

Copyright © Wispy Gorman 2011

Illustrations by Staffan Gnosspelius © 2011
www.gnosspelius.com

Printed and bound in Great Britain by T.J.I. Padstow, Cornwall.

'Fill your cheeks oh trumpeters! And let the jousting begin!'

Josephius (the monologues).

The stands were a mass of waving flags.

A hot day in the arena

This was the year of the *Hop-Pole Summer*. The year the pride of a nation rested upon the thin shoulders of a young man in a red baseball cap. A young man who wore glasses, and was given to leaning against things. A young man by the name of: Harry Hop-Pole.

'HOP-POLE! HOP-POLE! HOP-POLE!'

Harry glanced up. The stands were a mass of waving flags. All around the entire stadium people were on their feet. He waved back and the crowd went into a frenzy.

'HOP-POLE! HOP-POLE! HOP-POLE!'

Then he hefted his pole and walked out into the glare of the arena. He had come to jump.

How it all began. (Once upon a time…)

As Mrs Hop-Pole was being helped up the stairs, a woman with her hair tied up in a headscarf was kneeling at the bottom of the staircase, scrubbing the steps from a grey tin bucket of steaming water. She dipped in a filthy-looking rag, wrung it out, the suds seeping whitely from between the tightening creases as she did so, and slapped it back down on the next step. Mrs Hop-Pole was biting her upper lip against the discomfort. 'Alright love,' the old woman said. 'You'll be alright. It'll pass quickly enough. I remember my first, too - my little Albert.' Mrs Hop-Pole smiled at her kindness. 'Thank you,' she said, as the burly midwife helped to lever her up on to the next step.

And so it was, one misty September morning, as summer slipped effortlessly into autumn, that Mrs Mabel Hop-Pole gave birth to a baby boy. A short while later she was going back down the stairs with a child in her arms. And the old woman with the bucket had only reached the seventh step.

'Blimey! You was quick!' she said. 'Boy was it? Let's have a look at him, then.' And getting to her feet slowly, on account of her having rickety old knees, she reached out and stroked the little pink face peeping out of the blanket.

In thirty years cleaning the hospital steps she'd never seen anything like it.

'I've never seen anything like it,' she said. 'Out so quick his little face is hardly even all squashed up. They usually are, you know love,' she beamed at Mrs Hop-Pole. 'My Albert, he was all red and wrinkled - mind you he still is, bless him. But not your little feller. He's going to be a quick one, he is - you mark my words.'

*

A few years later Harry was at school. Quick he may have been, but the young Harold Hop-Pole was not what you would call a 'sporty' child. In fact he was never that interested in sports at all, preferring to lounge around on the edge of a field rather than run about in it.

The one exception to this was cross-country running where Harry was pleasantly surprised to discover that his naturally fluid running style enabled him to quickly outpace the pack, and allow him to spend the hour devoted to the 'hard-slog' of stamina-building exercise, sitting under an elm tree listening to the larks. He loved the song of the larks - that high-bright flittering that suddenly ceased, and then came again from somewhere else. Eventually his reverie would be disturbed by the rasping pant of aching lungs, and he would look up to see the first runners pounding uphill towards the trees. He'd wait till most of them had passed and then reluctantly get up and jog on again to finish somewhere in the lower-half of the field. He was not what you might call competitive.

In due course, Harry left school and took a job as a messenger-boy for a local newspaper. But he soon tired of that, and for a time he worked in a local baker's specialising in small cakes. Harry's job was to position the glacé cherries on top as the little white cakes passed down the conveyer-belt. It was not a demanding occupation, but then neither did it offer much in the way of fulfilment, and once again Harry moved on.

And now, for a while, the glass grows dim and Harry disappears from our view.

He reappears almost fully formed - tall, thin, bespectacled, and wearing a red baseball cap. Harry is now 24 years of age and is living in the converted attic of a Victorian terraced house with his new-found friend: Dick Scabbit.

Dick Scabbit

It was the first day of Spring and the two friends were chatting amiably as they strolled down the hill towards the café.

Dick Scabbit was a man who liked to be at the centre of things. Not unlike a film-director on location. This, he felt, was his destiny. To be there at the hub of events, sitting in a collapsible canvas chair.

The reality was somewhat different. He had no chair. There was just himself, and Harry, walking down through the park in the warm Spring sunshine. Scabbit was dressed as usual in his long black coat, his rubber-soled boots bringing a distinctive spring to his step and his long hair swinging against his shoulders as he loped along. They were discussing sheep.

Dick Scabbit loved all forms of wildlife. Even sheep. His favourite films were nature documentaries, the kind of thing that began with a family of gazelle around a waterhole as the great African sun rose shimmering behind them. And ended with one of them being eaten by a lion, while the same sun was going down in the background. But on this fine Spring morning he was a long way from Africa.

'I tried counting some the other day,' said Harry.

'Sheep?'

'You know - sheep jumping over fences, like they tell you to.'

'Rubbish anyway,' said Scabbit. 'I mean take that hedge there. No sheep could jump over a hedge like that! Even with a run-up.'

The hedge in question was seven-foot tall and bordered the churchyard of St Anselm's, which they were now passing.

They stopped and looked up at the hedge.

The warm morning sunshine was filtering down through the leaves. Winter was over, and Spring had come! Everything was filled with a sense of life and vitality. Harry was filled with a surge of vitality, too.

'Hold this a minute,' he said, handing his friend the red baseball cap he always wore, and to Scabbit's surprise he took a few steps backwards, then ran at the hedge and leapt clean over it, sailing a foot or so clear of the uppermost leaves of privet.

'Blimey!' said Scabbit.

'Ashes to ashes, dust to dust...' said the vicar who was conducting a funeral service on the other side.

The mourners were gathered around the freshly dug grave. The turves of grass, which had been cut away while the grave was being dug, were piled up to one side ready to go back on top, and it was on these that Harry landed with something of a thud.

He let out an: 'Omph!' as he hit the turf.

There was a collective gasp from the mourners, which caused the vicar, in his black cassock and white surplice, to turn and look behind him.

'Sorry about that,' said Harry getting to his feet and looking decidedly sheepish. 'Wasn't expecting...'

'Get out!' snapped the vicar. 'Can't you see these people are distressed? This is a sacred place! A place of peace and tranquillity!'

'Sorry,' said Harry, adjusting his glasses. He glanced apologetically at the ring of mourners. He'd seen one of them before somewhere, in the papers perhaps, the man had close-cropped white hair and pale blue eyes, and his biceps stood out through his coat.

Harry hurried out through the black wrought-iron gate, clicking it shut behind him.

'Where d'you learn to jump like that?' asked Scabbit.

'It's just something I've always been able to do,' said Harry.

'Oh,' said Scabbit, and at the time he thought nothing of it.

The sign of things to come

Outside the *Dog and Bucket* was the splendid new sign recently repainted at Brewery expense. The painting depicted a powerful, fierce-looking dog, part-alsation, part-anybody's guess, with its head in an orange polythene bucket. This was the new: *Dog and Bucket*.

Scabbit pushed open the door and they went inside. In an effort to attract new customers, or prevent old ones from leaving, Mickey Jakes, the landlord, had decided that a refurbishment of the premises was in order. And so, by the addition of a few comfy sofas and old armchairs, and the installation of a huge, new TV screen that filled half of one wall, the money was spent.

Sitting back in an old sagging leather sofa, with their feet up on the conveniently positioned coffee table, Harry and Scabbit found themselves looking up at the big screen.

'And as the contestants begin to arrive...'

There were scenes of people walking through airports, one man in particular seemed to be attracting a lot of attention.

The Dog and Bucket.

He was tall and tanned and had short blond hair. He stopped and smiled for the camera, and what a smile it was.

'Look at his teeth,' said Scabbit. 'My dentist would love me if I had teeth like that.'

'Who is he?'

'My dentist?'

'No, no - him up there.'

Scabbit shrugged and shook his head.

But moments later their question was answered:

'Jake Cranebilt.'

And there was film of him jumping over a bar with the aid of a long flexible pole.

He did it again and again all over the world, and wherever he did it people went wild.

But now he had a new audience. Harry and Scabbit supped at their pints, distinctly unimpressed.

'Is that it? Is that all he does?' said Harry.

'That's the trouble with our society,' said Scabbit, shaking his head. 'It encourages over-specialisation. You see, what makes a man happy is to be a well-rounded individual,' he rubbed his belly as he looked up at the screen. 'I mean look at this one here. He has spent the last 24 years... jumping over things... with a pole! Now that is not normal. That is not what nature intended at all. I mean there's animals that can do that kind of thing already. Take the kangaroo, for instance. Doesn't even need a pole.' He leant forward and took a good long gulp at his beer. 'And then there's all these people,' he gestured at the larger than lifesize figures on the screen in front of him. 'Look at them, they're treating him as if he's some kind of a genius.'

They were indeed. Jake was shown getting onto a bus. People clapped and cheered. Then he got off and they clapped again. Whatever the man did seemed to please them.

Scabbit gulped another mouthful of beer and set his glass down on the table. It was a bit of a stretch but he settled himself back on the sofa and was soon reclined in a more comfortable sprawl.

'And then there's us,' he said. ' - having a quiet beer on a Tuesday morning. Whereas those in the know, those who might be considered more *active* members of society. What are they doing? Chasing a man who jumps over things! Now, if you ask me, that is just bound to end in disappointment.'

He got to his feet and walked off in the direction of the toilets. He pushed at the door. Then remembered it opened outwards, and pulled instead.

He stepped up to the urinal and stared at the cracked white tiles in front of him. Where the tiles ended there was a line of encrusted dirt, and above the dirt, the whitewash began. On it, in a spidery hand, someone had written:

'All action springs from inaction.'

'I like the sound of that,' said Scabbit. *'All action springs from inaction…'* He turned to the sink to wash his hands. He worked the dispenser a couple of times but there was no soap. The water hissed cold and fast over his hands.

'Well, Dick Scabbit,' he said to the face in the mirror, 'I have a feeling that your hour has come…'

He dried his hands on a piece of tatty blue rag that had been thoughtfully provided for the purpose, and went back out into the bar.

On the big screen behind Harry's head, Jake Cranebilt was now meeting the Prime Minister.

'This is a great day,' said the Prime Minister. 'A great and historic day for our two nations. It is a great honour for us all to have Mr Cranebilt with us today.'

Scabbit looked up at the two grinning faces, and grinned back.

'Harry, my boy - I've just had an idea!'

'What's that?'

'Let's go get some food.'

The Café

They were soon ensconced at a table at the back of the café, where the swing-doors led into the kitchen, holding the little red menus in their hands. The menu hadn't changed, it never did but they turned over the greasy, plastic-coated pages just the same. It was all part of the ritual.

The waitress brought them over two scalding mugs of tea, folded back the top page of her pad and stood with her pen poised.

'I think we'll have…'

'Two full English?' she said, obviously in no mood to mess about.

'Er, yes. Thank you,' said Scabbit.

She leaned over, took the menus off them and walked off.

'I've been thinking,' said Scabbit, 'About that hedge you jumped over…'

'What about it?' asked Harry, blowing at the steam wisping from the top of his mug of tea.

'Well - that's given me an idea.'

Harry looked across the table at his friend.

Scabbit smiled innocently back at him.

'This idea wouldn't involve me by any chance would it?' asked Harry.

'As a matter of fact... yes! Yes it would!'

'Why does that not surprise me? Come on then, out with it.'

'I knew you'd like it!' said Scabbit leaning forward, smiling.

'Like it? You haven't even told me what it is yet!'

The waitress arrived with two very full-looking plates - eggs, bacon, sausages, a small pool of baked beans lapping at the rim, a heap of grey shiny mushrooms - the breakfasts in the café were nothing if not substantial.

'Ah, lovely,' said Scabbit rubbing his hands before he set to work.

'Well go on then,' said Harry, slicing into the white of an egg.

'Well,' said Scabbit, swallowing a nice, salty piece of bacon. 'What I was thinking - with you being so good at the jumping and everything. What about if we got you a pole? - then you could jump even higher.'

'Why would I want…? You mean like the guy we've just seen on the telly?' said Harry.

'Exactly,' nodded Scabbit. 'So what we need,' he said gesturing with a piece of hot-buttered toast, 'is a pole,' he took a bite, tearing it from between his teeth. 'And what you need is a manager.'

'I do?'

'Course you do,' frowned Scabbit. 'Can't get anywhere these days without a manager.

Excuse me!' he called to the waitress who at that moment was passing the end of the table carrying a stack of gravy-stained plates.

'More tea for my client here. And could you bring him a piece of that jam roly-poly?

 - we need to build your strength up,' he said more quietly to Harry.

The waitress affected not to have heard. She booted the swing-doors that led into the kitchen and disappeared from view.

'with custard!' he called after her. 'Please?'

The waitress reappeared and dumped the bowl on the table, along with a spoon that she put down next to it.

'Custard's run out,' she said and walked over to one of the other tables.

'So what do we do now?' asked Harry.

'You leave that to me,' said Scabbit. 'I know some people.'

The Syndicate

Long before its recent refurbishment, the *Dog and Bucket* had known grandeur. It had once been the famous *Station Hotel*. Back in its Victorian heyday* it had been a bustling establishment providing a comfortable resting place for the weary traveller. It was ideally situated, being connected to the station by a narrow footbridge.

The one disadvantage was that every time a train went past, the building and its occupants rumbled and shook, gradually settling again as the vibrations died away.

It was in just such a brief period of silence that Jim Griffin, his biceps bulging through the jacket of his suit, leant back in his chair and folded his arms. The chair creaked beneath him.

*F.E. - Ah, the Age of Steam! The reek of oil and piston, the surge of couplings, the great wheels beginning to turn…

I am the Fastidious Editor, by the way, nice to meet you so early in the story. Goodbye for now.

'So, tell us more about this *proposal* of yours.'

Dick Scabbit got to his feet. He had no notes. But then a great orator needed no notes. He just needed to be a great orator. 'Morning all!' he grinned.

The four faces looked back at him. He coughed.

'Once upon a time,' he began, 'this country was great. We controlled the seaways, we owned half the world, we built the factories, the ships and the...' (feeling the tremors beginning) '... the railways.' Perhaps it would have been better not to mention the railways.

Looking round the table that Thursday morning, Scabbit was aware of being somewhat out of his depth. After all, these men were: The Syndicate. And although their activities were largely of a clandestine nature, and therefore under-appreciated by the public at large, they were nevertheless highly influential.

Besides Griffin, there was Phlebbs of the local constabulary, his helmet on the table beside him, Charles Jaundice the Plannings Officer of the local council, who was unscrewing the cap from a very fine-looking tortoiseshell fountain pen, and Mickey Jakes, the proprietor of the *Dog and Bucket*, who was picking his nails.

The men round the table jolted and shook. Then waited expectantly as the train trailed away into silence.

Scabbit resumed: 'What we need, gentlemen, is a hero. Someone who will carry the flag of this once great nation. Someone who will give us... Victory.'

'So what you're saying,' said Griffin, 'is that our boy can beat the Russians, the Americans, and anyone else who happens to turn up. And get us a Gold Medal.'

'Right,' said Scabbit, nodding.

'So what's in it for us?'

Scabbit frowned.

'Where's the money?' said Griffin.

'Money?' He thought he'd explained all that. 'This isn't about money. It's about patriotism. It's about making Britain Great again. It's *us* showing *them* we can still win. If we decide we want to.'

Griffin snorted. Jakes frowned, and Phlebbs fiddled with the chinstrap of his helmet which had almost come loose at the point where it was riveted to the helmet itself and looked like it would need replacing some time soon. Perhaps he'd just put in for a new helmet.

'Right,' said Griffin. 'I'm...' and that was as far as he got because the 10.38 Express, taking them all by surprise, had rumbled right through the end of his sentence.

Silence.

Now they had a problem. None of the other members wanted to voice any objection to whatever it was their Chief had decided. Phlebbs had stopped fiddling. Jakes, unusually for him, was very still. It was Jaundice who broke the deadlock.

'So what's next?' he asked nonchalantly. 'What do *you* suggest Mr Scabbit?'

'Me?' thought Scabbit.

All eyes were upon him now.

'Well...' said Scabbit as he rasped his hand against his unshaven chin. Griffin was looking up at him enquiringly.

'Let's watch a film,' said Scabbit.

That threw them completely.

And in the consternation that followed Scabbit, never one to miss an opportunity, ran round drawing all the curtains.

'Mmmm,' said Griffin, settling down in his chair.

On the wall before them appeared the flickering image of a smiling face, short-cropped blond hair, blue eyes, perfect teeth and, as the camera panned backwards... a red and white vest.

'The American Jake Cranebilt...'

'This is the American,' said Scabbit forgetting where he was for a moment.

A couple of irritated sighs were heard to emanate from the backs of the viewers.

Scabbit swallowed.

The narrator continued:

'He began jumping over fences as a child. Out there on the family ranch in West Wyoming. At the age of ten he got his first pole.'

There was shaky footage of a kid with curly blond hair stumbling about in a barnyard with a red and white-striped pole. Suddenly the camera got jolted and two shadows appeared in silhouette on the ground, the taller of which seemed to be clouting the smaller one. 'The family moved to California where things were better. Then at college he fell in love with a cheerleader and joined the football team. And the baseball team. And the running club and the athletics....' There was another picture, a still this time, of a group of handsome young men all with short hair, all crouching down smiling into the camera. 'Since then he has gone on to dominate World Athletics especially in his chosen specialist event: The Pole Vault.

'The Pole remains my first love,' he was quoted as saying. 'All else comes second.'

'Arsehole,' said Griffin.

'And he is estimated to have earned prize-money and undisclosed sponsorship earnings in excess of ten million dollars.'

There was a sudden 'pricking up of ears' around the table.

'Mmmm?'

'How much is that in proper money?'

But the narrator went on: 'His only serious rival, if a man like Cranebilt can be said to have a rival, is 'The Great Russian', Tommaz Jinkski.'

And here the atmosphere of the film became a lot more sombre. For Tommaz didn't have such good weather. Neither when he was growing up, nor afterwards. Particularly afterwards. In almost every shot you could see how cold it was for Poor Tommaz because he would be standing there in his vest with the different letters on the front: CCCP, USSR, RUS and his shorts which would have been knee-length on any normal individual were like small briefs at the top of his huge legs. The man was a giant. But even a giant must sometimes feel the cold. And you could see how cold it was for Poor Tommaz, because while he was standing there in his vest and shorts, men in dark overcoats began to appear in the pictures. With hats on. First there was one. Then there were two. And after that there was always a little huddle of them off to one side, keeping an eye on Tommaz's progress.

'Like crows they are,' said Mickey Jakes, the landlord. 'Look at them in their nice warm coats just watching him. Bet they never done an honest day's work in their lives.'

And his comments struck some kind of chord, for the assembled company murmured in agreement, and even began to feel sympathetic towards the poor Great Russian.

The images ceased, and the film came to an end. Scabbit ran over and drew back the curtains.

'Just one question,' said Griffin, pushing his chair back from the table. 'Before we adjourn for today. What did you come to us for?'

An expectant silence hung in the air, suspended like the dust particles to be seen floating about now that the sunlight was once again filtering in through the grimy windows.

'Pride,' said Scabbit. 'England needs you. England needs Hop-Pole.'

Griffin chuckled, a noise like clinker being jiggled about in a tray. For besides being an utterly ruthless, entirely self-serving individual, Jim Griffin was a patriot at heart. And if he could do something for his country, without risk to himself, Jim Griffin was the man to do so.

'That's my boy,' said Griffin.

And Scabbit smiled back, relief flooding over him.

The training begins

'Relax,' said Scabbit. 'You're running like a rabbit, man.'

'A rabbit-man?' panted Harry. He was on his fifteenth lap of the under-fives playground and even the naturally fit Hop-Pole was getting slightly puffed.

Scabbit, meanwhile, was sitting on one of the swings, idly rocking back and forth.

Every so often, as Harry passed the swings, Scabbit would join in and bound a few paces after him, his long black coat flapping about him as he did so.

'A rabbit - you're all uptight. Relax. Lengthen your stride. Think of… the cheetah! Become the cheetah!'

'I'm starving. I need to eat.'

'That's it!' said Scabbit, excitedly. 'You scent your prey upon the wind. A wounded wildebeest, perhaps.'

'No, I'm starving. I need to eat. And not some wildebeest with a limp. I was thinking along the lines of a pie.'

'That's a start, I suppose. Wildebeest pie? OK, OK, let's call it a day.'

Harry ambled over and sat down next to Scabbit on one of the swings. The two of them sat there, legs outstretched, the chains above them creaking slightly as they rocked gently back and forth.

'When do we start the actual jumping?' asked Harry.

'The jumping? Ah yes, the jumping. Well we need a pole first, you see.'

'Where are we going to get one of those?'

Scabbit smiled secretly to himself. It was the smile of a man concealing hidden knowledge.

'You leave that to me,' he said.

The Syndicate meets again

The great grey river snaked and glinted in the sun. The trains came and went. And in the mysterious upper room of the *Dog and Bucket*, the talking had begun.

'Right, Scabbit,' said Griffin, pushing back in his chair. 'The floor is yours.'

'Well,' said Scabbit, getting to his feet. 'Since our last meeting we have begun preliminary training -'

'Who's supervising this training?' asked Griffin.

'I am,' said Scabbit.

'And what 'training' have you been doing? Running about in the park?'

'Pardon?'

'We're not *amateurs*, you know Scabbit. If this thing doesn't work, it'll be your head on the block. Is that clear?'

A sigh of relief came from Mickey Jakes, it being he who had introduced Scabbit to the Syndicate in the first place. Well that was one weight off his already overburdened mind. Yet despite the sigh, his forehead remained wrinkled and his eyes dull. Such were the pressures of running an establishment such as the *Dog and Bucket*.

'The thing is,' said Scabbit. 'Our Harry is a natural. A little light training is all that's required. That's the plan you see, we want him fresh as a daisy for the main event. Meanwhile all the other… jumpers, all his competitors, are getting up at five in the morning, pounding round racetracks, going on exercise bikes, consuming suspect substances, spending hours in the gym…

And what are they doing?'

'Getting fit?'

'No-oooh - they're tiring themselves out! And it could all so easily backfire.'

'It certainly could,' said Griffin meaningfully.

But Scabbit was undeterred. 'We meanwhile, are engaged in a little *light* training - so that when the time comes…'

He gestured expansively at his assembled patrons, and forgot what he was going to say next.

'There is one thing, though,' said Scabbit.

He looked round at the mildly curious faces.

'We need a pole.'

'You mean to tell me we've got this far. And you haven't got a pole?' asked Griffin leaning forward, his chair creaking as he did so.

'Well yes,' said Scabbit, ' - now you mention it.'

Griffin sighed and leant back in his chair. The chair creaked again.

'Tell me Scabbit, are you a man who *likes* to take risks?'

At that point a train rumbled past.

The shaking died down, and the dust was beginning to settle: 'Let's watch a film,' said Scabbit, and hurried to the curtains.

These new composite poles (a short film)

'The new generation of composite poles,' announced the narrator with feigned interest, *'has allowed the modern athlete to reach heights his predecessors never even dreamed of.'*

'Has it made them happy, though?' asked Scabbit.

Griffin looked round, irritated. Phlebbs just looked puzzled: 'What's a composite pole?'

'That's what we're going to find out,' said Jaundice, sarcastically.

'Ooh,' said Phlebbs. *'Intresting.'*

'These new composite poles are thermally extruded from hyper-extended multi-layer polymer chains which are then twisted and allowed to contract as they cool.'

'A bit like spaghetti,' said Phlebbs.

'In a process not dissimilar to the manufacture of spaghetti.'

'My God, I was right!' said Phlebbs.

'*Although on a much smaller scale,*' added the narrator.

'Well that's lucky!' interjected Mickey Jakes, his landlord's belly jigging up and down as he laughed.

'Will you stop interrupting the gentleman,' said Jaundice.

'Why? He can't hear us.'

'*This results in a lightweight pole which is both flexible and extremely strong.*

Whereas in the past, with a conventional pole, top athletes would be jumping around three and a half metres on a good day, nowadays even an average competitor would be expected to clear the five metre mark. And as a result the conventional pole has become all but obsolete in the modern era.'

'Right, well that seems clear enough. Let's just order one of them poles. Jakes you take care of it.'

'Just a minute,' said Scabbit. 'There's something else I want to show you.'

He changed over the films. The audience stirred restlessly in their seats.

The image of a leaf appeared on the screen. A leaf in black and white.

'Mmmm,' said Phlebbs thoughtfully, 'a black and white film.'

'Do you have to comment on everything we see?' asked Jaundice.

'Just making a routine observation.'

Then the camera panned backwards and the entire wall of the upper room was covered in leaf-patterned shadow. The leaves fluttered as if moved by a small breeze.

Then the trumpets sounded. And everyone jumped in their seats. Flat crazy trumpets bleating discordantly. And here was a picture of them now. Being blown by men with puffed out cheeks and strange floppy hats.

The trumpeters were standing outside a tent on the edge of a wood. It was a fancy-looking tent, shaped like an onion with streams of bunting trailing down to the ground all round it. Not the sort of thing you'd normally take camping at all.

Then the tent flaps opened and a man stepped out dressed in peculiar fashion (again not at all suitable for camping) with a crown on his head.

'*The King! The King!*' said the trumpeters and blew another flat brassy wail on the trumpets.

The King stepped up on to a little box that somebody had left outside his tent, and spread his arms wide for silence.

A train went past cruelly shattering the illusion and bringing the modern world jarring back in upon them.

By the time the train had gone, the King had gone also.

'*The flower of the French Cavalry are gathered this day upon the field of Agincourt…*'

Horses in fancy trappings were milling about, their riders rigid in their shining armour.

'*Opposed by the stout English bowmen.*'

(Daft grins peering from among foliage.)

'*With their Longbows.*

Made of stout English Yew.'

The film ended as the stout English bowmen lent back and their arrows were released…

Not the sort of thing you'd normally take camping at all.

'And that's what gave me the idea, you see?' said Scabbit.

He looked round at the blank, expectant faces. It was clear they didn't see at all. Phlebbs had stopped fiddling with his helmet, and was just staring at it vacantly, raising and lowering his eyebrows. Further explanation was needed.

'We will make the pole out of stout English Yew!' said Scabbit. 'That way we shall be invoking all the ancient glory and history of this island.'

'Whatever,' said Griffin. 'Jaundice - you better go with him.'

And so it was arranged.

'We'll take the van,' said Scabbit. 'I'll meet you in the café at ten.'

'What that awful place with stripey awning?'

'That's the one! Actually, make it eleven.'

Cometh the hour, cometh the man etc.

At 10.55 prompt, Charles Jaundice, for the first and last time in his life, pushed open the door of the café, and walked inside. He picked a table at random and sat down, which was a mistake since the table he had picked was right under the *'Specials Board.'*

The not unattractive brown-haired waitress, with her slightly pointy upturned nose walked over to him.

'I'll have a cup of tea,' he said, looking down at the menu, 'not too milky, not too hot, one and a half sugars…'

'Yeah, alright love. Just a minute. Got to do the *Specials Board* first haven't I?' She climbed up on to the bench where Jaundice was sitting, and trod on the pocket of his jacket. 'Sorry love.' She shifted her foot and began rubbing at the blackboard. A cloud of chalk dust spiralled slowly, settling on his hair and shoulders. Then in neat rounded writing she inscribed the *'Specials'* of the day: *'Soup of the day - pea and leek. Faggots in gravy. Pudding - apple crumble and custard.'*

'There that's better,' she said stepping down. 'Now. What can I get you?'

'Just a tea,' said Jaundice.

'Suit yourself,' she said, and walked off.

She brought back a mug of tea and put it down in front of him.

After a while the smells of tasty food wafting from beneath the kitchen doors began to work their insidious magic upon his nostrils and, without conscious decision, Jaundice found himself trying to attract the attention of the waitress. 'Er - excuse me,' he said, half raising his hand. She breezed past and gave the swing-door a particularly venomous kick. 'Be with you in a minute,' she called over her shoulder.

The doors swung back and she reappeared.

'What was it you wanted?'

'Ah, yes. I thought perhaps I might try some of your toast.'

'Try??'

'Yes, two slices please, not too thick, not too well done, with the crusts cut off and…'

'Alright, alright - I don't need to know how to make it. I just want to know what you want.' She sighed and wrote one word: 'TOAST.' And scored a couple of black lines underneath it.

'Is that it?'

Jaundice nodded.

In due course the toast arrived, golden with droplets of melting butter.

'Chef says you can cut your own crusts off,' she said, holding the plate tantalisingly out of reach. 'If you don't like'em - just leave'em on the side. OK?'

As she turned away she rolled her eyes. But by then Jaundice had raised the first slice of toast to his mouth and as he bit through the crisp surface, the warm butter delivered all that his taste buds had been promised. He drifted into a state of mellow contentment, staring absent-mindedly out of the window at the stream of cars and people passing.

Half an hour later a white van, with: *'Percy the Plumber'* painted on the side in big blue letters, pulled up outside. Jaundice watched it aimlessly. *'Percy the Plumber - your pipes is my business.'*

'*Your pipes is my business?*' frowned Jaundice, ' - but that's not even English!'

Then the door slid back and down stepped Scabbit. 'Oh my God,' muttered Jaundice.

'Come on Charlie Boy we're late!' yelled Scabbit leaning in through the door of the café.

Charles Jaundice was not an easy man to embarrass but on this occasion he flushed crimson. Right up to the tips of his ears.

'Charlie Boy!' sniggered a loyal customer, his spoon poised over a bowl of apple crumble and custard.

'Shut up,' snapped Jaundice. His chair scraped backwards on the tiled floor as he stood up.

'Eh-heh! Eh-heh! Eh-heh-heh! Charlie Boy!' shaking his head.

Jaundice gave him a scathing look, but the man was looking down into his bowl of custard at the time. He pulled open the door.

'Hey Monsewer!' said Old Nick the proprietor from behind

his till. 'Not trying to run off without paying are you?'

'Oh, right. Oh sorry,' said Jaundice becoming flustered.

'Now then, what did you have?' said the proprietor flipping back through the entries in the pad. 'Ah yes, two teas. Two toast, ' - not too well done with the crusts cut off and extra butter." Old Nick raised his eyebrows, then sighed through pursed lips. 'That was you wasn't it sir?'

'Yes! Yes! Hurry man.'

'You won't get no curly hair if you don't eat your crusts!' he said jocularly.

'For God's sake, man. I'm in a hurry!'

'Not bothered about curly hair then,' said Old Nick. 'Only trying to be friendly.'

He muttered to himself as he rang up the various items on the till.

'That'll be...'

Jaundice handed him a crisp note and pulled back the door.

'Thank you!' called the proprietor. *'Charlie Boy,'* he added as the door was swinging shut. Jaundice turned and glared.

'Come on. Jump in,' said Scabbit leaning across the front seat. Jaundice climbed up and sat down. The van lurched down off the kerb and they pulled away. As far as the traffic lights which were red. A few people crossed the road, a man with a barrow-load of cabbages bringing up the rear. Scabbit was fascinated by the antiquated wooden trolley the man was wheeling. 'Don't often see those these days do you?'

'What, cabbages?'

The lights changed and they were on their way.

The search for the perfect Yew

Jaundice-the-passenger looked at his new surroundings. A baboon was loping along the top of the dashboard.* Followed by a grey plastic elephant, which in turn was being pursued by three pigs and a cheetah. The cheetah was obviously from a different set of animals as it was much smaller than the pigs. And its feet were standing in a grey blob of glue. It was going to be a long journey.

'Animal-lover are you Scabbit?'

Scabbit turned to see if he was being made fun of. But Jaundice had regained his composure and his features were veiled by their usual reptilian calmness.

'What?' said Scabbit, one hand on the wheel.

'All these animals,' gestured Jaundice. 'That monkey for instance.'

*F.E. - *Ah, the baboon!*

'Monkey? What monkey? Oh, you mean the baboon.'

Jaundice rolled his eyes. 'A *baboon*.'

'That's right,' said Scabbit. 'They're very social animals, baboons. They live together in large troops and help each other out with the grooming and such.'

They took a tight corner and Jaundice swung over to lean on his shoulder. Scabbit gave him a sidelong glance. He was not accustomed to close physical contact, least of all from a Plannings Officer. Jaundice shuffled back into position.

'So, who's Percy?' he asked.

'Who? Oh, Percy - he's my friend. He's a plumber.'

'Yes, I rather gathered that.'

'He sold me the van.'

'Humph,' replied Jaundice.

'He's got a new van now. Got a new slogan, too. It says: *'Water water everywhere? 'Don't be a drip! - call Percy!'*

Jaundice sighed, and began massaging his temples.

They passed the last of the shops and were then in a residential area - rows of red-brick terraced houses, then a building site shuttered off behind plywood fencing: 'Prime Site for Development'. Jaundice smiled wryly to himself, remembering the heart-warming sight of a demolition ball swinging at the end of a chain and a cloud of tumbling masonry.

Gradually the houses became fewer and further apart, set back from the road behind hedges of privet and the odd clump of buddleia. Soon they were out in the country. Jaundice stared out of the windows at the monotonous green of the fields. In some were wheat and in some were barley and in some were black and white cows. But to Jaundice it was all the same, a dreary absence of town. 'What a waste,' he thought to himself, shaking his head. 'Not a building in sight.'

'I love the country!' said Scabbit winding down the window. 'It's in us all isn't it, eh? - that yearning to get back to our peasant roots? To be close to nature and all the animals.'

A waft of particularly pungent farmyard manure surged in through the open window. Jaundice wrinkled his face in distaste.

The search for the perfect Yew (cont'd)

Eventually they arrived at their destination, the village of Fillingbourne Stoutly. It was a quaint little village with a few thatched cottages, a church, a pond with white ducks on it, and an inn: *'The Croaking Frog'*.*

'Stupid name for a pub,' said Jaundice getting down from the van.

'Well it's near the pond, I suppose.'

They crossed the street and went into the churchyard. There was a black wooden lychgate over the path and beside it, a venerable old yew tree, its branches twisted and furrowed with age. They walked straight past it and up to the door of the church, which appeared to be locked.

*F.E. - of course so much depends on a name does it not? I am reminded of a rather racy establishment I used to frequent in my youth: 'The Horse Dropping with Fatigue.' Just on the edge of the gallops, it was.

To the left of the door was a black metal hoop jutting out of the wall. Jaundice pulled down the lever. They waited, looking up at the ancient crossbeams arching above their heads. Nothing happened.

'Here let me try,' said Scabbit. He grabbed the lever and cranked it up and down a few times. 'Must be broke - '

Then a mournful tolling began: 'B-Bong! BONG! B-Bong! BONG!'

'Someone's bound to hear us now.'

Someone had. The sound of footsteps, hurried, frantic footsteps scampering towards them. Then a small old man with wild hair and a limp appeared, holding a little blue cap in his hands.

'Is it the invasion? Have they come?'

He squinted up at them, twisting the little blue cap nervously in his hands as he spoke.

'What?? Have who come?' asked Jaundice

'I must away off home and rouse the village!'

'No wait, wait!' called Scabbit after him. 'It's only us.

We're… we're… We mean no harm.'

'No time! No time!' he shouted over his shoulder as he hobbled off down the path.

All of a sudden the clamour of the bells ceased. Silence descended. It was a peaceful country churchyard once again.

'Strange,' said Scabbit.

'No stranger than anything else we've seen round here,' observed Jaundice.

Scabbit glanced at the parish noticeboard.

There was a *Coffee Morning* on the 20th. And a *Bring and Buy Sale* on the 23rd.

'Isn't that nice,' he said. And then he saw it. 'Look! Look! The Fillingbourne Yew!' For pinned up on the noticeboard was an L-shaped newspaper cutting which told the history of *'The Fillingbourne Yew.'* The ink was faded and the paper yellowing but the picture was still recognisable. 'That was it! The one we passed by the gate.'

'The thought had crossed my mind,' sneered Jaundice.

But Scabbit ignored him, and read on eagerly: *'This Yew. This Great Yew has stood rooted to this very spot for nigh on a thousand years. It was here before the Normans trod these shores. And may have been…'*

'1066,' said a voice behind them.

'Are you the vicar?'

'No, I'm the new curate.'

'Oh, hello. I'm Dick Scabbit,' he said smiling and leaning forward to shake his hand. 'And this is my… this is…'

'Jaundice,' said Jaundice stepping forward. 'Charles Jaundice.'

The new curate reached into the folds of his cassock and produced from his cavernous pockets a large black bundle of keys. He bit his lip as he sifted through them.

'Nope. Nope. N-Yes that's it. I think,' and he bent and poked the key into the lock. 'Nope.'

Scabbit read on: *'The Yew we see today was one of a pair that stood either side of the path forming a gateway to the parish church, the other, its pair, died of woodworm in 1912. And from that date on, this last surviving yew, thought to be the biggest and most robust in the country, was christened: 'The Widow' by the local parishioners. And the name has stuck: 'The Fillingbourne Widow."* Isn't that nice?' said Scabbit. 'Fancy your 'other half' dying of woodworm eh, Charlie? Terrible thing. Mind you, if I was married to you... Does it hurt, woodworm? Do you think?'

'Nope,' said the curate.

There was a loud click and the door creaked back on its hinges.

'Ah,' said the curate. 'I thought perhaps it was that one!'

He pressed a switch underneath which was written:

LIHGTS

and all the lights came on.

'Well,' he said, opening his arms. 'This is the nave, these are the pews where the faithful all kneel, that's the altar up there (where I do my bit), the pulpit, the stained-glass window showing Our Lord on the morning of the resurrection. There he is there you see - the stone rolled back and that strange kind of light around him - particularly beautiful that is on a nice spring morning when the sun shines in through the window. It faces east, you see, catches the early morning sunlight.' He stood there with a beatific expression on his face smiling up at the window. 'Mmmm,' he sighed.

'Ah, oh yes now this is interesting!' and he led them over to an old board that was hanging on the wall. It was a list of names with dates beside them, etched in neat copperplate script. 'This is a list of all the vicars the parish has had since the early twelve-hundreds.'

'Makes you think, doesn't it?' said Scabbit, as he stood reverently in front of the board. 'They had some funny old names in those days didn't they?'

'Would you like me to show you around the rest of the church?' the curate asked eagerly. 'There's Lord Filbert's tomb, and all the brasses - you haven't seen those yet.'

'Well it's the Yew we've really come to see.'

'Oh well, never mind. Another time perhaps. I'll go and fetch the vicar for you.'

When they came up the steps out of the church the curate let out a sigh, 'Oh no,' he said. 'It's the Activist,' and hurried off to find the vicar.

'The Activist?' said Jaundice, frowning.

Standing in front of the ancient yew was a small, thin protestor, with a placard and tangled-looking shoulder-length brown hair. 'SAVE OUR YEW!' it said on the placard. As he saw them approach he began to chant: 'Save our Yew! Save our Yew! Yew!-Yew! Save our Yew!'

'Will you shut-up,' said Jaundice.

'Save our - '

'SHUT!

 UP!'

The Activist looked taken aback.

But then he seemed to regain his courage:

'Free country. Anyway can't build here, it's against the law!'

That was the wrong thing to say. Entirely the wrong thing to say.

'Don't you start quoting the law to me you little squirt!' said Jaundice. 'I could build an abattoir in your front room if I wanted to!'

'Not big enough!' said the Activist. 'Anyway the council wouldn't let you.'

'The Council? I *am* the Council!' screamed Jaundice.

The veins on his forehead were pulsing lividly and spittle flecked the edges of his mouth. Striving to regain some kind of control he spoke very quietly: 'Scabbit, get rid of this... specimen before I shove his placard up his - '

'No need to get nasty,' said the Activist. 'I was going anyway. Can't stand around here all day. Got other things to complain about.'

And off he went, carrying his placard over his shoulder.

'Karma's going to get you!' he called back through the hedge.

'Rrrrr!' growled Jaundice. 'You little ba...!'

'Ah, there you are!' said the curate smiling. 'The vicar will see you now.'

The vicar was in his study. A pleasant, west-facing room where the sunlight came late in the day, and the trials and tribulations of life but seldom.

The room was furnished with soft rugs underfoot, leather-bound books round the walls, and a grandfather clock in the corner which ticked methodically as the large flat brass pendulum swung backwards and forwards, backwards and forwards.

The vicar had the air of a man who had just been woken up from a pleasant drowse in a comfortable armchair, and was none too happy about it. He scowled beneath wayward eyebrows. The cat which had been sitting on his lap, jumped down to the floor, stretched along the length of its back and curled up on the rug instead.

'This is Mr Jaundice, and Mr...'

'Scabbit,' said Scabbit. 'Dick Scabbit.'

'Yes, and er, they are very interested in our ancient Yew Tree,' said the curate.

'We only want a strip off it. Well a couple of branches. Side-shoots would do even,' said Scabbit. 'In fact a good long side-shoot would do just fine.

As long as it was a stout one.'

Jaundice looked at him irritably.

'I think I can handle this, Scabbit. After all, that was why Mr Griffin sent me. Why don't you just… wait in the graveyard.'

'Right, well. If my assistance is not required,' muttered Scabbit, 'I'll leave you two to it, then,' and with a nod at the vicar, out he went.

'Well,' said Jaundice. 'This is a lovely room you have here,' he gestured at the clock and the rows of books, and finally at the armchair the other side of the hearth from where the vicar himself was sitting. 'May I?'

The vicar yawned and nodded as Jaundice sat down.

'Well,' said Jaundice. 'This is nice, Persian if I am not mistaken?'

'Affectionate little thing isn't she? Aloof, as all cats are but -'

'I was referring to the rug.'

'Ah.'

'And that clock over there, very nice - very expensive.'

'Perhaps you would be kind enough to get to the point, Mr Jaundice.'

'Well as my colleague inadvertently let slip we are, let us say, *interested* in your tree.'

'And what form would this 'interest' take?'

'Mmmm,' said Jaundice, sensing that he was nearing familiar ground.

Scabbit, meanwhile, was wandering around in the churchyard. Someone had left a jam jar with a few wildflowers standing in front of one of the graves. The flowers were blue and white, and their heads drooped slightly against the glass of the jar. Some of the graves were overgrown with tufts of grass, and there were patches of lichen on the stones. And there were others, more ancient still, where the headstones, almost unreadable now, had been taken up and were stacked against the churchyard wall.

Scabbit walked over to the yew tree and sat down on the bench in its shade. A blackbird was hopping about among the graves. It stopped, turning its head on one side, as if listening to something. Scabbit found himself staring at the ring of yellow around its eye.

And the voice, when he heard it, was gentle and somehow familiar: *'When time has passed, and time has gone, and all we've loved has come and gone...'*

He got up and ran back into the vicarage.

'Give me a pen! Give me pen!'

'What?'

'Give me a pen. I've gotta have a pen! - You've got to have a pen!'

Jaundice sighed and reached inside his jacket pocket and handed him a very fine tortoiseshell-patterned fountain pen.

'Mind the nib,' he said handing it over. 'The top unscrews,' he added sarcastically.

Scabbit snatched up one of the blue, gold-embossed hymn books, that was lying on the side, ripped the top off the pen and began scribbling.

This was a new experience for Dick Scabbit. He had never before handled such a fine writing instrument. It was a new experience for the pen, too. It was accustomed to elegantly shaping the signature of: *Charles S. Jaundice* on Certificates of Planning Permission and other very important documents, so the paths it followed were well worn and familiar. But now it was in Scabbit's clutches, and that was an altogether different experience.

'When time has passed,' it scratched. 'and time has gone…'

'B-b-but! I must protest!' said the vicar. 'That is one of our hymn books you are writing on!'

'Shhh! Won't be a minute: 'and all we've loved…''

'They were part of the bequest of Lady Filbert herself!'

But Scabbit couldn't care less about Old Lady Filbert - he was away with the muse and she was far more captivating, if a little more elusive. She glanced at him from between some trees, the wisp of a veil, the trail of her dress disappearing through trees…

'…has come, and gone.'

And all of a sudden, she had.

'Gone,' he said, and shouldered past them out into the graveyard.

They found him there half an hour later, sitting on the bench with his head in his hands. 'Gone,' he said. 'All gone.'

'What's gone Scabbit?'

'Never mind,' he said with a glassy look in his eyes. 'You wouldn't understand.'

The blackbird began singing, a few bright little trillings of song, to try and lighten the atmosphere. Then realising this was an altogether more sombre occasion than even it was used to, it stopped, and watched events from the silence of its perch.

'Where's my pen?' demanded Jaundice.

'Your pen... oh your pen,' said Scabbit handing it over.

'We've got the tree!' said Jaundice.

'Have we?' said Scabbit disinterestedly. 'That's good.'

But Jaundice was not to be deterred by his lacklustre tone and went on enthusiastically.

'A new bequest has been arranged! Thanks to you really. You gave me an idea with those hymn books.'

And then, in a fit of uncharacteristic generosity, he added, 'Come on, I'll buy you some lunch.'

Some Lunch

They ducked beneath the heavy lintel of *The Croaking Frog* and stepped inside. It was dark and wood-beamed, and there were flagstones on the floor. In the gloom behind the bar stood the landlord, round of face and flaxen-haired. He eyed them, unspeaking, for a few moments. Then suddenly seemed to become animated.

'Welcome!' he said. 'Come through into the Pot Room!'

He motioned them through the doorway. Sprawled across the flagstones in front of the fireplace was a large dog of the mastiff kind.

'Now that is a big dog,' said Scabbit. 'Look at the size of him.'

'Aye he's asleep, though - won't hurt you. Just as long as you don't go waking him up suddenly.'

They sat down either side of the long black table, taking care not to scrape their chairs so as not to disturb the sleeping hound. It was quiet in the Pot Room, very quiet. The only sounds were the gentle respirations of the sleeping dog.

The landlord returned with two mugs of frothsome ale.

'There,' he said setting them down. 'That's our local brew. Now, what about something to eat? We've got: Toad in the Hole, Shepherd's Pie... or Pheasant. Or I could maybe make you a sandwich?'

'Pheasant for me!' said Jaundice. 'What about you Scabbit? What are you having?'

'Shepherd's Pie,' he said stolidly.

*

After a very fine lunch featuring two substantial helpings of Shepherd's Pie, half a trug of boiled potatoes, and a few wet obligatory greens, Dick Scabbit was feeling more like his usual self - well-earthed and substantial. He leant back and patted his belly.

The landlord, who had been watching them closely throughout the meal, approached the table.

'Enjoy the Shepherd's Pie did you, sir?'

'Very nice, said Scabbit, as he handed up his empty plate.

'And what about you sir?' said the landlord, turning to Jaundice. 'Enjoy the pheasant, did you?'

'A very fine bird,' agreed Jaundice, who was still in an unusually affable mood.

'Shot it myself, so I did,' said the landlord. 'Hope there wasn't too much lead in it for your liking? Anyway I always says a bit o'lead don't do you no harm. Wouldn't eat it myself like. But the customers they seem to enjoy it. And I likes to please. Oh, yes, I likes to please.' He beamed down at them. 'And you didn't mind the jaw marks, I hope? Not too many of those little ribs popped in?'

'What? What are you talking about?'

'He's talking about that bird you just ate,' said Scabbit.

'That's right,' said the landlord nodding. 'You see he's a grand hunting dog is old Jess, and he and I have brought down many a pheasant, but he's a loopy old thing. And sometimes I think he forgets he's got a bird in his jaws at all.'

At the mention of his name the hound swung its collosal head towards them, drool spilling from its sagging jowls.

'Enjoy the pheasant, did you sir?'.

'Of course!' said Scabbit, his good humour now thoroughly restored. 'A hunting dog, eh? Charlie,' and he slapped the table. 'Ha! Looks a bit dribbley though wouldn't you say?'

'Well,' said the landlord, shaking his head. 'We can laugh about it now, since we're all old friends, but when he brought the kill back to me...' (Jaundice groaned at the mention of the word: 'kill') 'and dropped it on me boots, it was all acovered in his dribble it was, all the little feathers all plastered together.'

'Ha ha ha,' said Scabbit. 'Lovely dog!'

'But I think I cleaned most of it off, I did. But it took some scraping, I can tell you. It was all slimey and sticky. Now you'll be having some pudding, of course?'

'Ah yes, pudding!' said Scabbit, rubbing his hands.

'I'm not hungry,' said Jaundice.

'Ah, come on, Charlie Boy. Anyway you're paying! Might as well indulge! Might help to wash it all down, eh? Ha!'

Some time later, a plumber's van was seen to round the curve past the Alms Houses and head for the open road. There was only one man whose services were indispensable to them now and they had been told where to find him.

The Last Pole Carver in England

'He lives in a hut in the middle of the forest,' the landlord had told them. 'Just ask when you get there.'

'Ask who?' said Jaundice.

'Anyone - they all knows Chindlin Bob!'

*

There was a large sign by the side of the road: *'YOU ARE NOW ENTERING THE ANCIENT FOREST.'*

'This must be it,' said Scabbit.

So they parked the van in a convenient lay-by and walked over to inspect the sign more closely.

YOU ARE NOW ENTERING THE ANCIENT FOREST. Tread carefully for things are not what they seem. (Not by a long way, matey.) Do not cackle or behave frivolously (e.g. chuckin acorns and such) for this will surely disturb the shy woodland creatures what herein do dwell. Indeed, you may have a strange feeling that you are being followed. Do not worry about it! - this is just your past catching up with you! Now get in there and have a nice walk.

(This was writ by a young wood-elf, Stumpy by name, Stumpy by nature. Thank you.)

'What's all that supposed to mean?' snapped Jaundice.

'Well...'

'Anyway who are we going to ask?'

'A passer-by?'

As it turned out they did not have long to wait.

*

It was not a lyrical voice but it did have a certain quality of exuberance about it:

'My love she loved me-HEE! My love she loved me.

My love she loved me-HEE! My love she loved me!'

And round the corner came a shepherd. At least he looked like a shepherd, walking as he did with the aid of a large crook, which he shook in time to the joyful ditty he was singing.

He came face to face with the two strangers, whom he seemed not to have noticed until he stood right in front of them, at which point he emphatically planted his staff and sang out lustily:

'My love she loved me-HEE! My love she loved me.

My love she loved me-HEE! My love she loved me!' and then he bowed.

Jaundice shook his head and got back in the van.

'Very nice,' said Scabbit. 'Now I wonder if you can help us. You don't by any chance know where the pole-carver lives do you?'

'Ah you be wantin Chindlin Bob...'

'That's right, yes.'

'Now he's hard to find is Chindlin Bob. He's always in his hut, you see. And his hut is hard to find.'

'So where is his hut?'

'Why, in the forest of course! Deep in the middle of the forest.'

'Thank you,' said Jaundice acidly, from the window of the van. 'That really is most helpful.'

'Anytime,' said the shepherd smiling up at him - it was a simple, gap-toothed smile. 'Anytime is the right time for me-HEE!...'

'Where? Where in the forest?' Scabbit shouted after him.

But the shepherd just went on singing.

'Anytime is the right time for me-HEE!...'

*

It was quiet on the edge of the wood when the shepherd had gone. The trees were still and silent. Then the foliage parted.

And a little black-faced sheep appeared. It looked up at the van, with a half-bored, half-curious look, and then trotted down the side of it.

The leaves moved again and out came a second. And a third. This one was scarcely more than a lamb. Jaundice leant on the window, watching them go past. 'One… Two… Three… How many more of them are in there?' he frowned. 'Four… Five…'

He began to yawn…

'Seventeen… Eighteen…'

He yawned again, and slid lower in the seat.

And still they came.

Eventually the last sheep emerged from the undergrowth and ambled along the side of the van. There were no more.

Scabbit banged on the windscreen. Jaundice opened his eyes.

'Can't sleep now Charlie! Come on let's get going.'

They climbed over the stile and went into the wood. After about an hour of aimless meandering, they realised they were lost. A small figure stepped out from between the trees. He was dressed all in green. He stopped a few yards away and peered at them round a tree-trunk.

'Are you the Sheriff's men?' he asked.

'Are we what?'

Then he was gone.

'Wait! Wait!' shouted Scabbit. 'We think we might be lost.'

But all they heard were scampered footfalls on fallen leaves, and then nothing. From then on they had the eerie sensation of being followed, but when they turned there was nothing behind them, just a feather eddying downwards on the still air. Scabbit went over and picked it up. It was a grey feather, with flecks of brown and black. He twirled it between his fingers, still squatting down on one knee, and looked around at the silent ranks of motionless trunks.

'I hate woods,' said Jaundice petulantly and he kicked, and scuffed up a few leaves.

'Sshhh!' said Scabbit. 'Listen - isn't that a woodpecker?

I've always wanted to hear a woodpecker. In a wood.
 - a real wood-pecker in a real wood!'

'Will you shut… up. Please,' said Jaundice.

'- Thank you.'

Then they both heard it: 'Nut-nut nut… nut-nut-nut…'

'There it is again! Did you hear it?' asked Scabbit excitedly.

'Of course I heard it. I'm not deaf! Any fool could hear that.'

And they walked in the direction of the sound. As they got
closer they realised that the sound was not: Nut-nut nut…'
but:

'Mmmm-hmmm nut nut nut…'

'Mmmm-hmmm nut nut nut…'

Then they stepped into a clearing, and there in front of them
was a wooden shack made of various planks and patched up
oddments of timber. It was a singular construction. But then
its creator was a singular man.

The door of the little shack was open and inside, with a pile of wood-shavings round his feet, and a few in his straggly white hair, was Chindlin Bob himself: The last pole carver in England.

'A-hum. Good afternoon Mr Bob,' said Jaundice at his silkiest.

The old man's eyes narrowed.

'You be wantin something,' he said accusingly.

'Well actually yes, as a matter of fact we were wondering - '

'Ah wandrin' were ye? I heard ye wandrin.
You're not from round 'ere are you?'

'Well as a matter of fact - '

'Nah, nah. Thought as much to myself I did. When I heard you bumblin' and stumblin' through the wood.'

'Was that you? With the feather?' asked Scabbit.

'Ah, the feather...' said Chindlin' Bob, closing his eyes and gazing ecstatically towards the heavens.

'The feather,' he murmured. 'Many's the long night I've sat here… What feather?'

Jaundice let out an exasperated sigh.

Then drawing Scabbit to one side: 'We are wasting our time,' he whispered between clenched teeth. 'The man is quite clearly deranged in some way. Even if he does make nice poles.'

'Poles is it, you're after? You'll find no finer pole-maker this side of the Great Estuary.'

'The Great Estuary?' said Jaundice. 'What Great Estuary? We're nowhere near a bloody estuary? What are you talking about?'

'Precisely. You'd hav'ee to go a long way indeed to find a pole-maker who can turn as fair a pole as Chindlin Bob. Though I do say so myself.'

'Look I'm getting fed up with this,' said Jaundice storming out. The door swung shut behind him.

The air had the dry, slightly resinous smell of freshly planed wood. And in the narrow confines of the hut, two men now faced each other. One with a beard full of sawdust. One without.

'So,' said Scabbit. 'Will you make us a pole, then?'

'Aye, that I will.'

'Thank you,' said Scabbit and he turned and ducked under the lintel of Chindlin Bob's strange little hut. He turned in the doorway. 'We'll get the wood delivered to you then.'

'Aye. The Fillingbourne Widow.'

'How did you know about the Fillingbourne Widow?'

'Ahhh. Many's the long night I've longed to get my hands on the…

The vicar told me.'

'The vicar?'

'Tele-phooone,' he said and closed the door.

The Syndicate meets again - a progress report

The door was closed in the upper room. The Syndicate were in session.

'Well?' asked Griffin. 'Did you get it?'

Jaundice flinched at one of a series of painful memories. He had not suffered from migraines for many years, but since the visit to Fillingbourne Stoutly they had returned with a vengeance. He put his hand to his temples as the room began to shake.

'Yes,' nodded Scabbit, as the train went by.

'So when's it going to be delivered?'

'It'll be ready by the end of the month.' He had in fact been told to return *at the first glimmer of the new moon*, but he decided to withhold that particular piece of information.

Griffin just grunted. 'I hope this 'Bob' knows his business. This better not be some second-rate pole we're getting off some daft yokel.'

'Ooh no,' said Scabbit. 'He's the finest pole carver in all of England.'

'Well he better do a decent job, that's all I can say.'

'There is just one thing,' said Scabbit hesitantly. 'Where are we going to put it when we get it back? It needs to be somewhere safe.'

'Somewhere in penetrable,' muttered Phlebbs pursing his lips and frowning down at the table.

'We could stick it in the cellar,' said Jakes.

'Will it be safe down there?' asked Scabbit.

'Nothing gets out of my cellar that I don't know about.'

'Except botulism,' said Jaundice, half under his breath

'That wasn't the cellar, it was the kitchen! Anyway it was unproven.'

'Only because we 'unproved' it!'

Griffin sighed irritably and tapped very gently upon the tabletop. 'You know, sometimes I feel I'm surrounded by a bunch of overgrown schoolkids.'

His words had a chastening effect upon those gathered around the table who sat up straight in their chairs, put their hands in their laps and looked down at their thumbs. Big thumbs, in the case of Mickey Jakes, who began picking the dirt from under his nails.

'Jakes!'

He jumped in his seat.

'Sorry Chief.'

'Is your cellar safe?'

'Oh.Yes, Chief.'

'Thank you.'

Jakes grinned at Jaundice, who ignored him and sniffed disdainfully.

'And stick an extra lock on it,' said Griffin.

A smile spread slowly over Jaundice's face.

'Phlebbs, you can see to that.'

'New lock, sir. Very good, sir.'

There was a pause.

'I'll get one of those new locks, sir,' he added as a somewhat delayed afterthought. 'One of those *combination* locks.

With numbers,' he added.

'I don't care what you use. As long as it's foolproof.'

'It'll be foolproof, sir. I'll test it myself.'

'Good, well I think that's everything. So what are we waiting for?'

The Coming of Sister Saul

It all began with a note through the door.

'Sister Ignatius Saul will be in your area, next Friday.'

About a week later, Harry and Scabbit returned from a not particularly gruelling training session to find another note lying on the doormat:

'Sister Ignatius Saul called while you were out. She will return.'

'Who is this Sister Ignatius Saul?' asked Harry.

'I suppose we'll find out when she comes back, won't we?'

*

It was morning and the doorbell was ringing.

Harry groaned and rolled out of bed. He went downstairs still wrapped up in the duvet.

The doorbell rang again.

'Alright, alright - I'm coming!'

He opened the door and there on the step, in a little grey cap, was a postman.

'Oh,' said Harry. 'I thought you were my friend.'

The postman looked at the dishevelled hair and the crumpled pattern of the duvet, and reached his own conclusions.

'Got a parcel for you,' he said, and held out a brown packet. 'If you could just sign here.'

Harry scrawled across the pad he'd been handed.

'I hope that's OK,' he said. 'I haven't got my glasses on.'

The postman shrugged. 'It's all the same to me, mate. I just need a signature.'

Harry felt the parcel. It was soft and squashy, he was curious. He tore open the brown-paper packing and a vest felt out. A huge vest that unfolded itself of its own accord.

Harry blinked and stared at it. Even without his glasses on he could see it was a vest of unusual proportions. When he tried it on it came down to below his knees. He shuffled along towards the hall mirror and was standing in front of it when the doorbell rang again.

With some difficulty Harry retraced his steps to the front door and opened it. Three women stood on the doorstep wearing black hats. They were arranged in height order with the tallest on the right. It had been the tall one who had operated the doorbell. And it was she who now spoke:

'Why does God let bad things happen to good people?'

Harry looked down at his vest. They all did.

'Do you fear death?' said the second.

'No it's just the wrong size' said Harry. 'They've sent me the wrong size!'

'What is that you are wearing?' said the third, and evidently most practical of the trio.

'It's a vest. I think they've sent me the wrong one.'

'Would you like one of our little magazines?'

'How will that help?'

'Perhaps you would like to come along to one of our meetings?'

'No thank you.'

'Sister Ignatius Saul makes lovely cakes,' said the smallest of the three.

The tall woman smiled modestly.

'Oh, so you're Sister Ignatius Saul,' said Harry.

'So you've heard of me then, young man.'

'Well yes, you keep putting notes through my door.'

'Not just your door. We've done every door in the street. And all the streets round about.'

'Lovely cakes,' said the small one again.

'No thanks,' said Harry. 'I can't eat cakes. I used to work in a bakery you see, it put me off.'

'It's never too late to repent,' said Sister Ignatius Saul,

solemnly. 'What about a donation? Would you like to make a donation?'

'What for?'

'For the cakes.'

'But I don't want any cakes.'

Stalemate. The two sides looked at each other, each realising that, for the moment at least, no further progress was possible. Sister Ignatius Saul sighed.

'Whatever has happened, has happened for a reason,' she said.

'I'll buy that if you will,' said Harry.

He went to shut the door but a hard-booted foot was wedged in it. Sister Ignatius was taking no chances.

'If all else fails. Try putting it in a boil-wash. It might shrink.'

'Thank you. I might just do that,' and with a sigh of relief he closed the door and went into the kitchen to put on the kettle.

It was an ancient whistling kettle, blackened and dented with age but still, when the steam escaped the vent in the lid, capable of a satisfyingly tuneless whistle. It began as a hissing and lisped its way to a crescendo. Harry lifted it off the hob with a cloth.

The doorbell rang again.

It was the postman. He took in the apparition before him - Harry in his overlong vest. And again his face was a study in world-weary tact.

'Oh, it's you,' said Harry. 'I thought it was…'

'Nevermind. Nevermind,' said the postman handing him another parcel. 'Just sign here - I think we both know the routine by now.'

Harry signed.

'Alright, mind how you go,' said the postman.

'Thanks,' said Harry, turning away with his new parcel in his arms. This one was soft and squashy inside. Just like the last one. Feelings of curiosity, wariness, and *déjà vu* drifted like clouds across his being.

'DISPATCHED IN HASTE,' was stamped in black ink across the corner of the packet.

Harry tore it open.

Inside was a vest.

'That's more like it. Look it comes down to my waist - just like a normal vest!'

He was delighted. It was something he could run in. Not just shuffle.

An hour or so later Scabbit returned from some unspecified early-morning errand and soon he and Harry were sitting opposite each other, drinking mugs of tea. Harry was lying on the sofa with his feet up on the armrest, while Scabbit was in a sagging armchair, his legs stretched out in front of him.

'So,' he said. 'How's it going?'

'It's been a strange morning really,' said Harry.
'My vest arrived though.'

'That's good,' said Scabbit. 'All we need now is the Pole.'

The Subtle Art of Strategy

A goods train screeched past, bound for the coast. Long after the 'loco' had passed, the brown, box-like carriages were still rattling, clattering past the window. Eventually there was a sort of: 'Whaup!' of air and the last one was gone, trailing along at the back as if in a hurry to catch up. But of course it never would.

'Lot of carriages on that one,' observed Phlebbs. 'Goods train, that was. You can tell by the carriages. No people in them. Just goods.'

'Right,' said Griffin. 'Back to business. Now the next thing - I want to know who the judges are, who their families are, where they live, everything about them.'

'No, no, no,' said Scabbit. 'You don't understand.'

'Don't tell me my job, sonny,' he glared. 'I've been nobbling judges since you was in nappies. So don't tell me... how to nobble... a judge.'

'But the point is to win this *without* nobbling the judges.'

Griffin frowned. Then raised his eyebrows as the sheer novelty of the proposal left him speechless.

It was Jaundice who broke the silence. 'That's all very well,' he said, 'but surely there's no harm in oiling the wheels so to speak - just for... *insurance* purposes.'

'What wheels?' asked Phlebbs.

'Oh for God's sake,' said Jaundice. 'Where were you?'

'When?'

Griffin cleared his throat, and then began tapping his finger very lightly upon the dark polished oak of the table. Order was restored.

'Anyway, Scabbit. Shouldn't that pole be ready by now?'

The Return of the Pole (when Scabbit returns to Chindlin Bob's to pick up the Pole)

It was a pleasant journey and the company was better, because this time Dick Scabbit was alone. No Charles Jaundice. Just himself, and the animals glued to the warm black plastic of the dashboard. It was a fine, early Summer's day, and they raced along with the windows wound down and the warm country air wafting in.

He parked the van in the lay-by by the side of the road, and climbed over the stile. As he entered the forest, Scabbit looked up at the high, arching splendour of the beech trees. The sunlight shone down through the green-lit leaves, creating a pattern of dappled light and shade. A squirrel scampered ahead of him. An unseen bird was singing. And in no time at all he found himself on the edge of the clearing.

Chindlin Bob was in his shack. He had his back to the doorway and was applying the finishing touches to a finely-crafted pole, working away with a spokeshave. Scabbit stood for a while and watched the craftsman at work. The gentle swish of the shave, the white wood peeling thinly away, the smell of sawdust and resin on the air. The old man was so engrossed in his work he seemed unaware of Scabbit's presence.

Scabbit knocked gently on the door frame.

Chindlin Bob froze. Then turned round very slowly.

'What you doing creeping up on me like that? Could have given me a heart attack. I'm an old man, remember. Even if I does look so sprightly and all.' And with two bounds he crossed the floor, gripped Scabbit by the arm, and pulled him inside. Then, very gingerly he peeped outside again, glancing quickly left and right. 'Came on your own did ye? Where's that weasel you brought with you last time?'

'Who? Oh, yes him. I left the weasel behind,' he laughed.

'Now there's a man not to be trusted' I says to myself as soon as I clapped eyes on him. I did so. His face is too pointed and his eyes too, too…'

'Ferrety?' suggested Scabbit.

'Errrrr-um,' uttered the old man, twiddling the wisps of white hair on his chin. 'Ummm. Aye - Ferrety'll do.'

Scabbit, standing ankle-deep in wood-shavings, with his hands in the pockets of his black coat, looked around at the various tools hanging from the roof of the hut.

'Yourself, on the other hand, I says to myself: 'Now here's an honest yeoman."

'Oh, thank you very much,' said Scabbit. 'That's very kind of you.'

" - he should be worth a guinea or two,' I thinks to myself.'

'What?'

'Now you come along here and sit down on this here box. I'll be making a b-rew. Will I make one for y-ou?'

'Thank you,' said Scabbit. ' I would like a brew.'

So the two of them sat down on upturned packing cases either side of the black wood-burning stove and drank the strongest, darkest tea Scabbit had ever tasted. They chatted aimlessly about this and that, about life and the wood, and the wood and life, while gradually, one by one, the birds ceased to sing and the wood grew quiet and dark all around them.

'I had hoped one day to have a son,' said Chindlin Bob, staring into the flames. 'To pass on my trade, my dying craft. But my poor Mary, she was carried away with a fever, and after her there never was another.' A tear fell from the old man's face, and landed on the back of his claw-like hand. And in the darkness of the fire, Dick Scabbit pretended not to see it.

'Well,' said Scabbit, after a decent interval of fire-gazing. I should really be getting along now. It's late and I'm not entirely sure of the way.'

'Just turn left and follow the path. Saves blunderin about in the wood. But if I were you I'd wait till morning. Dawn is the time to be leaving. There's a pallet in the corner over there. You can sleep on that.'

Within minutes the old man was asleep, his snores rhythmic as a rasp running over dry, cross-grained wood.

Scabbit went outside and stood in the clearing looking up at the stars. There were millions of them. He tried joining them up, making shapes out of them. What a shame all the constellations had already been named. He would have been good at that. The wind breathed gently through the trees.

'Just turn left and follow the path.'

So he did. And in fifteen minutes he was back at the van.

'I had hoped one day to have a son.'

The van had a special rack on the side designed for the transportation of long pipes. Scabbit reached up and slotted the pole in the rack, then he pulled down the clips to hold it in place, and drove away. It really was the perfect means of transportation. Except that the pole was about five feet too long, so even while he gripped the wheel and attempted to concentrate on the road ahead, he was aware of the pole in the periphery of his vision. It was like being a beetle with one, long antenna.

The Pole Bearer

Scabbit pulled in at a truck-drivers café in the middle of the night. He drank a black coffee from a white paper cup.

'Far to go?' asked the man behind the counter.

'Back to the city,' said Scabbit.

He dumped the paper cup in the bin by the door. 'Thanks,' he said and went down the steps and across to the van.

As Scabbit approached the city, a tightness began to clutch at his belly. It wasn't hunger or tiredness even. Just the sense of being back in a different world, a man-made world of concrete, and street lights and shopfronts and houses. But something in the world he had left had touched him. Something of the trees in the greenwood still lingered about the fringes of his consciousness. And yet here he was back in the city.

By the time he reached home it was already light. The street lights were on but the light they gave out was feeble and yellow, a mere shadow of their nocturnal brilliance. Scabbit parked the van under the arch of the railway bridge and turned off the engine.

He sat for a while staring at the bricks of the bridge and listening to the engine tickering quietly as it began to cool down. No sense trying to sleep now. He decided to walk down to the café.

A window on the world

Old Nick the proprietor was reading the paper. This was his favourite time of day, when the café was empty, the radio played quietly in the kitchen, and the streets outside were darkened with dew. He had a cup of tea on the counter beside him. The newspaper was crisp and newly printed. The dry, dark smell of the ink mingled pleasantly with the warm aroma of the tea. He read and sipped, and sipped and read. And as the level of the tea sank lower in the cup, so his knowledge of the world's events rose accordingly. By the time his first bleary-eyed customers began to arrive, looking haggard and dishrevelled, fresh from their beds, Old Nick would already be abreast of the latest happenings in the world at large. And therefore in an unrivalled position, to share his in-depth knowledge of news, comment, and informed opinion.

This then, was his routine, which took a bit of a jolt when the door opened and in walked Scabbit. Old Nick looked up at the clock. For a moment he was caught off guard.

'You're up early Scabbit,' he said, and then recovering quickly ' - or haven't you been to bed yet?'

Scabbit explained that he had in fact lain down briefly many hours ago. 'But that was in a cabin in the woods with an old man snoring.'

'Did he bump his head, did he?'

'No, it wasn't raining,' said Scabbit quickly.

Old Nick was impressed. This kind of repartee was unheard of at that time of the morning. 'Tea or coffee?' he said, bringing things back down to earth again.

Scabbit ordered a coffee and sat in the window sipping it.

Across the road from the café was a fishmonger's. A man in shiny white boots was winding down the stripey blue and white canopy. It unfurled jerkily as he cranked the handle. Then he went back inside. He reappeared a few minutes later, carrying armfuls of some floppy grass matting. The grass was bright, and green, and fake, and he spread it carefully on the sloping stand in front of the shop.

Scabbit sipped at his coffee and watched the fishmonger setting out his stall. First came the ice. Buckets of it. Then the fish. Buckets of them. He tipped out a shoal of sardines and began arranging them painstakingly in the shape of fan. Then came the cod. Big and pinkish grey, with bristles on their lower lips and glaucous eyes.

And last of all, the *pièce de résistance* - an immaculate salmon, huge and wise and, recently poached from a Scottish loch where its ancestors had gone to spawn for generations. But not anymore. For now it lay beached and lifeless on a bed of sprats and whiting.

Then came some fake plastic parsley, poked in here and there, to add a further touch of greenness. (The fishmonger hummed as he did that.) And then whatever was left - a headless halibut, hacked about and mutilated almost beyond recognition, a few stray prawns and a slippery handful of squid - the fishmonger had second-thoughts about them, scooped them back up into the polystyrene box from which they'd come and hid them round the back, together with a bleeding slab of tuna and then another box of cod which had somehow become separated from its fellows - the perils of swimming in a different sea.

After three double-espressos, Scabbit was glassy-eyed and twitching. And the last of the cod were laid out on the ice.

Waiting was the worst part.

But now it was over.

That long journey through the night, the unfamiliar surroundings, the net drawn dripping from the water…

Then up went the grey metal shutter and the door was opened. The fishmonger was ready for business.

So was Scabbit. He unclipped the pole from the side of the van, walked round to the *Dog and Bucket*, and lent on the buzzer. *'M.Jakes Esq. - licensed purveyor of intoxicating liquors of all kinds and in quantities he deemeth sufficient.'*

'WHA?' came the muffled, distorted voice. Jakes was a man who slept late.

'It's me - Scabbit.'

'Scabbit? Oh, Scabbit. I'll be down.'

A few moments later there were footsteps, then a jangling of keys and the sliding back of bolts, and Mickey Jakes appeared in a purple and white striped dressing gown.

'One pole,' said Scabbit and tilted the Pole towards him like a knight dipping his lance in salute (or the barrier on a level-crossing gate closing).*

*F.E. '- the barrier on a level-crossing gate closing.' - what a fine simile this is! Ah yes, many's the time I've stood by the side of the track waiting for a train to go past in my shorts. I am thinking here of my youth, you understand.

Jakes took the other end of it and shuffled backwards into the hallway.

'Mickey?' came a voice from above. 'Mickey? Who was at the door?'

'Dick Scabbit, love. He's come round with a pole.'

'Oh.' And over the banisters appeared the cheerful face of Mandy Jakes. She was wearing her curlers. 'Hello Mr Scabbit!' she called down.

'Morning Mandy!'

The two men continued along the corridor with the pole. Soon they would come to a corner and that would require a discussion on how best to proceed, but for now everything was straightforward.

'Oh, Mickey?' came that kindly, strident voice again.

'Yes love?'

'Why has he come round with a pole at this time of the morning?'

'Long story, love.'

'Oh. Righty ho, then!'

Safety in numbers

It was mid-afternoon when Constable Phlebbs came into the bar.

Furtive glances from the faces slumped over the counter.

'Pssst! Pssst!'

An old man in one of the comfy new armchairs stopped snoring and sat up.

But Phlebbs was in good humour:

'Don't mind me, gentlemen. I'm not in an arresting mood!

Huh-huh-huh!'

And they all laughed back at him. And winked at each other.

Jakes scowled at them, but Phlebbs, as usual, was oblivious.

'I have here the supplies you requisitioned,' he said, and dumped a heavy plastic carrier bag on to the counter of the bar.

'Here is the lock,' he said taking it out of the bag.

'You type in the number here, you see… one - nine - seven… six!'…

and Hey Presto, Open Sesame…' he picked the thing up and began rattling it.

'Mmmm,' he frowned. 'There seems to be some problem with the mechanism.'

'Try: 'One - nine - *six*… six!" suggested a suspicious-looking character helpfully.

'No, you're wasting your time with those things if you don't know what you're doing,' said Jakes. 'Hey Babbings, come and have a look at this lock will you?'

Babbings shrugged and came down the bar. He was a small, thin man in a flat cap, his hands in the pockets of a tattered grey jacket. He looked down at the lock and smiled as he picked it up in his skilful hands.

'Bloody amateur could open this one.

If so inclined,' he added. 'Look you apply a little pressure here. Just enough to hold it apart. That disengages the catch, you see.

Then you try the numbers. Now the trick is, you have to start from this end. And we try the numbers: one, two, three... Now when you get the right number - you feel a slight give in the mechanism. You got that?

Then you do the same for the other three.

And there you go!'

There was a whirr and a click.

'- hey presto - it opens!

Like I said, bloody amateur could open it.

Here you try.

But you must start from this end. Otherwise you'll be there all day. And time is of the essence in these things - ' he coughed nervously, suddenly afraid he might perhaps have revealed too much. But he needn't have worried. Phlebbs was still engrossed in opening and closing his new toy.

'Much obliged to you... Babbings,' he said at last, with a big smile on his face.

'You're welcome, sir,' said Babbings. '*What goes around comes around!* I always say. Who knows? Perhaps some day you'll be able to do me a favour!'

'Mmmm,' said Phlebbs thoughtfully, and lifting up the flap at the end of the counter, he followed Jakes out through the bar and down the steps to the cellar.

*

No sooner had they gone out than the front door opened and in stepped Sister Saul and her two companions.

'What den of iniquity is this?' she demanded indignantly.

'It's *The Old Dog*, miss.'

'You should be ashamed of yourselves. Give me a donation immediately.'

Then, in a slightly quieter voice, she spoke to her black-bonneted assistants: 'Sisters, go round with the tins while they're still in a stupor. This hellfire stuff wears off after a while and we want to strike while the iron is hot.

You there, little man,' she said to Babbings, 'turn out your pockets - I'm sure you've got some loose change in there.'

'Now look here,' said Babbings, 'I don't mind giving you no donation - out of the kindness of my heart - but what goes in my pocket, stays in my pocket,' and he felt for his set of picklocks just to make sure they were safe.

'And what's that man doing over there?'

'That's old Erasmus - he's asleep, miss. That's why he's snoring. He only snores when he's asleep, you see?'

'A-sleep? A-sl-eeee-p? At three o'clock in the afternoon?'

'He was up all night miss, couldn't sleep. He's insomniac.'

But Sister Ignatius Saul, once embarked upon a course of action, was not to be thwarted. And she clocked him a beauty on the top of his head with her black umbrella.

'OUCH!' he said sitting up, rubbing his head.

'Ooooooh,' said his sympathetic companions.

And all the while, the tin was going round briskly.

'That hurt!' said the old man, still rubbing his head.

'The Lord will always forgive a sinner,' smiled Sister Saul, and she jangled her tin in front of his nose.

*

Meanwhile down in the cellar…there was a strange gasping noise in the darkness.

Then a stifled snigger.

It was a while before Phlebbs realised his companion was laughing.

It was a while before Jakes could speak.

'You know where we are?'

'We're in your cellar,' said Phlebbs.

'No, we're in the… Pole Vault!'

'The what?'

'The Pole… Vault!'

Phlebbs looked at him blankly, his head on one side, as if tilting it in that direction might somehow improve the thought-process.

Jakes held the lantern up to his face, and tried again.

'The 'vault' where we keep the 'pole'! You see?'

'Hur, hur hur! The Pole-Vault! Huh-huh-huh!

I like that!

Huh-huh-huh!

I like that!'

And he did. In fact he liked it so much he shared it with everyone he met.

An emergency meeting

'What's the matter with these bloody trains?' said Griffin. 'They on strike or something? Haven't heard one in ages!' he turned his gaze away from the silent tracks. 'Anyway, what was it you wanted to tell me?'

'Well...' said Mickey Jakes. 'It's like this...'

And then the rumbling began.

'What???' shouted Griffin. 'I can't hear you!'

The train trailed away into the distance.

'It's gone - missing.' Jakes swallowed.

'What???' asked Griffin, incredulous. 'How can you lose a fifteen-foot pole?'

'I reckon it's the Russians,' said Jakes. 'The Russians have half-inched it from under our noses. I'm certain of it.'

'This ain't the Russians,' said Griffin, getting to his feet. 'I'll tell you who's behind this,' he said, staring out over the rooftops. 'This is that lot North of the River. Henderson's behind this. I can smell him. The Big Fat... *Piano-Player.*'

He turned away from the grime-covered windows.

'You better pay him a visit, Scabbit. Say I sent you. Say we want our pole back. Is that clear?'

Scabbit nodded.

'You know where they hang out, don't you?'

The Skipping Maid

The Skipping Maid on a Friday night. Scabbit stood in the dark of the alley outside the pub. From within came the sounds of revelry and laughter. Someone was playing a piano, punctuated by the occasional sounds of breaking glass, and voices raised in song. Scabbit distinctly caught the words: *'Fifteen men on the dead man's chest - Yo-ho-ho and a bottle of Best!'* He shuddered.

A cold gust of wind blew down the alley leaving a beer can rattling in its wake. Above his head the inn-sign was swinging, creaking back and forth on its rusty hinges.

Scabbit drew in a long deep breath. Then pushed open the door.

Everything went quiet.

All heads turned towards the newcomer.

'Evening,' said Scabbit pleasantly. He tried to smile, but his face was too tense. He walked up towards the bar, across a mile or two of beer-stained carpet, and stood in front of the three gleaming taps. The barman raised an eyebrow.

'I'll have a…' Scabbit scanned the brass oval labels affixed to the front of each tap. '*Strong*', '*Strong*' and '*Extra Strong*'. He frowned, somewhat non-plussed. 'What's the difference between…' A murmur went round the clientele. It was an angry, threatening murmur. The kind of murmur one might expect having just jolted a beehive. 'OK, I'll have a pint of… *Strong*,' said Scabbit.

'Which one?' said the barman.

The murmur came again.

'The middle one,' said Scabbit decisively.

The murmur subsided.

The barman pulled back on the tall wooden-handled tap and the beer came hissing into the glass.

Scabbit took the pint and looked round for a table. The only space was in a sort of alcove between the piano and the fireplace. The noise was deafening and the heat was unbearable.

He picked up a beermat and turned it over.

'Answer this question correctly and you could win one of a hundred and fifty immaterial prizes!

Ohhh?' said Scabbit to himself.

'Who invented the sponge-bag?

a) the Greeks
b) the Romans
c) Tutankhamun
d) Cleopatra.'

He took a good long pull of his beer and wiped the froth from his upper lip on the back of his sleeve. 'Got to be Cleopatra hasn't it?' and felt in his pockets for a pen.

By then the music had stopped and the pianist, in his shabby grey suit, came over and joined him.

'Evening,' nodded the Pianist.

'Evening,' said Scabbit.

'Mind if I join you?' and he squeezed himself into the alcove beside Scabbit.

'Not at all. Be my guest.'

'So you've crossed the river then?'

'Yes,' nodded Scabbit.

'How was it?'

'Grey, murky.'

The Pianist nodded. 'Sounds about right.'

They chatted companionably for a while. The regulars of *The Skipping Maid* soon returned to their Friday night revelry, and their presence, it seemed, was no longer noticed. Scabbit thought the time was ripe for him to steer the conversation round to the topic that was troubling him.

'Have you heard anything about a pole?' he asked.

'A pole, you say? What kind of pole?'

'A jumping pole.'

'A jumping pole, eh? Now why would a man cross the river on a Friday night to find out about a pole?'

'I come from Griffin...'

'Ffffffffffffff,' hissed the Pianist. 'I wouldn't mention that name in here if I were you. There's some in here who don't much care for Mr Griffin.'

'Well anyway he - '

'Who, Griffin?'

'Yes. I thought you said…'

The eyebrow arched up enquiringly.

'Well anyway,' said Scabbit. 'The message is this: What he proposes is a truce.'

'A truce?'

'But only until after *the event*. After that all normal hostilities will be resumed.'

'You're sure about that?'

'Those were his actual words.'

'They were? I don't want any back-sliding on that one.'

Scabbit shook his head emphatically.

'Well in that case,' continued the Pianist. 'Allow me to make a few discrete enquiries.'

'Thank you,' said Scabbit 'That's - '

'Oi! MOPPIT!' he bellowed across the room at one of his henchmen.

'YOU HEARD ANYTHING ABOUT A POLE?'

The Widow Returns

A few days later, they were gathered in the upper room of the *Dog and Bucket* when there came a frantic knocking at the door.

Griffin looked at Jakes.

The barstaff were under strict instructions never to interrupt the secret meetings that took place in the upper room. For they were secret meetings and no one was supposed to know they were there. The knocking came again. 'Mr Jakes! Mr Jakes, sir!' It was Allsop the barman. 'It's me, Allsop! Allsop the barman! Pardon my interrupting your secret meeting with the other gentlemen, but there's a note just arrived, sir. A young street urchin ran in with it, said it was very important, and then ran off again as fast as his little legs could carry him.'

There was a small scuffling noise and a note was pushed under the door.

Jakes bent over and picked up the note.

'Message for you here Scabbit,' he said straightening up.

'Bloody lumbago.'

Puzzled glances.

'Must be some kind of code,' said Phlebbs quietly.

Jakes rubbed his lower back, wincing as he hobbled over towards the table.

"The Widow Returns,' it says here. That mean anything to you?'

'Ha!' said Dick Scabbit. 'Come with me gentlemen.'

They went downstairs. And down again. Down into the very bowels of the old hotel, where they gathered in front of the cellar door.

'Constable Phlebbs,' said Scabbit. ' - if you would be so kind?'

Phlebbs stepped forward. He frowned, with the effort of memory, and then tapped in a four-digit number.

'One - nine - six... six!' There was a loud clunk and the door swung open. 'Look at that - it opened!'

The others pushed past him into the cellar. The air was cool and had the pleasant aroma of fermenting malt. There were ranks of wooden barrels on either side. And there in the corner, leaning against the wall, was the pole.

'Ahhh,' sighed Mikey Jakes. 'I knew it'd come back.'

'Did you?' said Griffin. 'You didn't seem quite so sure last week.'

'But is it the same pole?' asked Jaundice.

'That's true,' said Phlebbs. ' - it could just be any old pole. I mean we wouldn't know, would we?'

A train rumbled quietly overhead.

'Only one way to find out,' said Scabbit decisively.

'What's that then?' asked the Constable.

'Take it to Harry.'

'It's time I met this boy anyway,' said Griffin.

When Harry meets the Griffin

This was the first time Harry had been the other side of the bar and Scabbit was leading the way. Round and round they went, stair after stair.

'Must keep you fit climbing this lot,' said Harry, as Scabbit laboured ahead of him. The latter grunted by way of reply. Eventually they emerged on to a landing and paused in front of a door.

'What are we waiting for?' asked Harry.

'I'm trying to get my breath back.'

Scabbit knocked on the door.

'Who is it?' came a voice from inside.

'It's me, us - Scabbit.'

The door opened and Scabbit ushered Harry inside. 'This is...'

'Here, don't I know you?' said Griffin.

'Er - don't think so,' said Harry recognising him instantly.

'Yes, wait a minute - you're the little blighter that jumped over the wall into my mother's funeral!'

'Er -O-ooh. Oh yes. Now you mention it.'

'I do. I do mention it,' and he stepped towards Harry and eyeballed him.

For some reason Harry did not back away, but held his gaze, steady and unflinching.

Griffin grunted, and turned away, satisfied. There were very few men who could hold his gaze, and none of them south of the river. He nodded. 'Well the boy can jump, anyway. I seen him in action.'

There were smiles and nods from the attended gathering.

' - right over that bloody wall...' said Griffin through his clenched teeth. He wandered over to the window and stared out at the rooftops, his hands clasped behind his back. In his mother's day, there would have been plumes of smoke streaming from each of those chimneys. Thin wisps of grey that would be bent by the wind and blown eastwards against the greying sky. But not anymore. Now they all had gas central heating. The world was changing. Even in his lifetime he'd seen it change. This was the end of a dying age. And he and his men were making one last stand before it all faded into memory.

Griffin turned and spoke again.

'Now listen, Son. There's a lot of us here who've gone to a lot of trouble for you,' as he said the last two words he jabbed a fat finger in Harry's direction. 'So don't let us down, right?

Oh, and another thing.

Good luck, my Son.'

The Tournament Commences

The games began with an opening pageant. The competitors processed round the arena holding their poles aloft, their national flags flying from the tops of the poles. It was a moving and colourful spectacle.

Jake Cranebilt led the procession as he was the reigning champion, behind him, and attracting quite a few cheers, came 'The Great Russian', Tommaz Jinkski, then a bunch of no-hopers and then at the back of all these, last of all, came Harry Hop-Pole.

'Why's our boy at the back?' asked Griffin, angrily.

'Because nobody knows who he is yet,' said Scabbit. 'But they will. Just wait till the jumping starts.'

'Yeah, well. Disrespect I call it. DISRESPECT!' he bellowed at the top of his voice, batting his programme on the head of the man in front.

'I say, mind out!'

'What?' said Griffin. 'What's your problem?'

One of the no-hopers, who was passing at the time, smiled and waved back at him.

'Cheeky git,' said Griffin. 'Ah, here comes Harry. We're watching you Harry me boy!'

Harry looked up and grinned, and then yawned, holding up the procession momentarily while he changed hands with his pole so he could cover his mouth. He switched hands again and the procession moved off.

The Jumping Starts:

In his little glass box, high above the arena, the Announcer sat all alone. His was a god-like view. Way down below him, ant-like figures moved industriously about their business. They were getting ready for the next event. He glanced down at his programme: The Pole Vault.

On the table in front of him, was a fat packet of sandwiches in greaseproof paper. He unwrapped them carefully, feeling the hunger stir within him as he did so. Cheese and onion. Cheddar, naturally. Matured for months in the time-honoured way, on a shelf, in a barn, in Somerset.

Beside the sandwiches, was the large rounded bronze grill of the microphone - his only conduit to the world below. He clicked the switch to the 'ON' position. The red light came on: 'Transmit.' He did so.

'THE POLE VAULT!'

He clicked it off again. And picking up the sandwich in both hands, he took a large bite out of it, and sat back chewing.

He was a man who said little, but said it loud.

The box where he sat was bare and utilitarian. Its comforts were few. Cold in winter, and hot in summer. But the views... the views were astounding. And in case they wanted improving, he also had his 6x30 binoculars. By the foot of his chair he had a thermos flask of lukewarm, milky tea, and in his jacket pocket - a treat for later, a round, and slightly sickly chocolate biscuit, wrapped in red tin foil. While behind him, on the wall, was his old green mackintosh, hanging limp from a rust-blackened nail. This, then, was his domain.

The views were magnificent. The banks of slow-drifting clouds, the bushy-topped trees on the far blue hills, the rooftops of the city nestling in the curve of the great river, and there in the distance the old power station. Gaunt and obsolete now - a monument to the industry of a previous age. He bit into a piece of onion and looked around him in contentment.

*

Meanwhile, in their box at the back of the stands, the Commentator and the Archivist sat side by side in their deckchairs. Theirs was a far more homely box, not bare and austere like the man above's. The Archivist had his big dusty books strewn about his feet: *Pole-Vaulting Through The Ages, Pole Vault Stats, Jump Stats, Jumpers and Jumping, Pole Position,* a few back issues of *The Pole*. And if all else failed: *The Book of Common Knowledge* - while the Commentator had a cup of tea. In a delicate bone china cup with wild roses on it. There were also a few most welcome parcels of provisions sent in by well-wishers. Though these had yet to be explored. The Commentator set down his cup and peeped out of the window.

Down in the arena, there was the bustle of organised activity. The stewards had cleared away the debris from previous engagements and were now setting up the jump. It was fairly straightforward: two uprights, a crossbar, and a nice soft blue bed to land on.

Four attendants carried the bed in, one at each corner, the two at the front shuffling backwards, the bed sagging in the middle. The spectators waited patiently. At last the preparations were over. It was time for the jumping to begin.

First up was the Frenchman.

The Commentator leant forward in his chair. 'Who's this jumping?'

'JACQUES FLECHE!' came the voice from above.

'He's French,' added the Archivist.

'Ah, yes' said the Commentator. 'Nicknamed: *'The Arrow,'* I believe.'

'That's right,' confirmed the Archivist, with a confident nod.

Flèche came running in, dipped his pole at the last minute, which curved and catapulted him over the bar, where he landed gracefully on the bed behind. He got to his feet amid muted applause.

But apparently he'd overstepped the mark and the jump wouldn't count.

Laughter broke out among the stands.

Though this was quickly silenced by the Announcer, his voice echoing from conical loudspeakers all over the arena.

'AND NOW, THE MOMENT WE HAVE ALL BEEN WAITING FOR...

IT'S J-AKE C-RANE-BILT!'

Applause and lots of it.

Jake ordered the bar to be raised. And then raised again.

A small official carrying two large tablets walked out on to the track.

'Who's that little moses guy down there?' asked Jim Griffin from the comfort of his fold-down seat.

'Shhhh - he's the height official.'

'Why's he so short then eh? Haaaaa-h! Height-official! Ha ha haaah!'

The little man raised the tablets as high as he could above his head.

The tablets lit up.

5.85

'FIVE METRES... EIGHTY-FIVE!' confirmed the voice from above.

'Five metres eighty-five?' said the Archivist. 'If he gets this it'll be a new World Record! Cranebilt's trying to wrap the whole thing up with a single jump!'

'Five metres eighty-five - what is that in feet?' asked the Commentator.

'That's a big leap,' said the Archivist. ' - that's about... twenty foot. Give or take.'

Jake waited for the applause to subside. Then levelled his pole and ran.

He was noticeably faster than Jacques Flèche, dug in his pole which curved back under his weight and flung him upwards, and just when it seemed he was going to hit the bar he arched his back and sailed clear.

'HE'S DONE IT! HE'S DONE IT! JAKE CRANEBILT HAS SET A NEW WORLD RECORD!'

'But has he peaked too early?' murmured the Commentator into the privacy of his mouthpiece.

But up in the stands they had their own questions.

'Can our boy cope with that?' asked Griffin anxiously.

'Have faith thee of little...Don't worry,' said Scabbit, ' - he's out the back eating oranges.'

'Oranges?'

Next up was Jinkski.

'I read about him the other day in the paper,' said the Commentator. 'You know what they call him? *Jumping Jinkski!*'

'Well, well. Whatever will they think of next,' said the Archivist.

'Funny isn't it - *Jumping Jinkski!*'

Jinkski pounded down the track, his pole juddering as he jabbed it into the ground, let out a grunt and launched himself upwards. He lacked the panache and lithe athleticism of the American but it was a good solid effort, (*'Workmanlike'* the papers were to call it the next day) and he cleared the bar at five metres eighty, ever so slightly in the American's shadow.

One by one the others jumped. And failed.

'AND NOW, REPRESENTING GREAT BRITAIN, WE HAVE HA-RRY HOP-POLE!'

'Who?' asked the Commentator.

'Harry Hop-Pole. He's our new… er jumper.'

'Oh, I didn't know we had a new jumper. Is that him down there in the red cap and glasses?'

'Now wait a minute,' interrupted the Archivist. 'Here's an interesting situation. Besides Jinkski and Cranebilt the others have all failed to qualify. Hop-Pole only needs to clear the bar to qualify for the final!

But I don't suppose Hop-Pole will realise that.'

But he had.

Harry left his pole resting against one of the railings and wandered over towards the height-official. He smiled down at the little man. Words passed between them. The height-official threw up his hands and was seen to gesture round at all the spectators. Spectators who had paid good money to see this event. And could now hear nothing of what was being said.

The height official held up his tablets.

'THREE FOOT FOUR!'

'Three foot four?' said the Commentator. 'But that would be the lowest jump ever recorded! Is that right?'

A moment of silence.

(The Archivist leaned over the side of his chair, frantically scrabbling for the very comprehensive *Jumpers and Jumping*.)

Then, quick as a flash, back came the answer:

'Yes. The previous record lowest jump was Walter Bingham in 1908.'

'Thank you.'

The satisfying thump of a thick book being closed.

'Walter Bingham, you say?'

The Archivist sighed and reached for *J and J* again.

'Not to worry,' said the Commentator. ' - I think you said Bingham. Or perhaps it was Bongham?'

The crowd stirred restlessly as Harry ambled back to the starting position and hefted his pole.

'Yes here we are: *'Bingham, Walter - 1908 - recorded a jump of three foot, six inches under a cattle-gate in Richmond Park."*

'Uh-huh. That must have been before they had electric-fencing.'

'Mmmm, yes.'

'When did that come in?'

The Archivist sighed and looked over the side of his chair. 'Off the top of my head - I really couldn't tell you - I'd have to look that one up.'

'Nevermind, nevermind - I'm sure one of our viewers'll know.'

'I said I'd look it up OK! Don't want some busybody calling in telling me my job.' He had *The Book of Common Knowledge* open on his lap and was hurriedly flipping through pages.

'Oh look, here comes Hop-Pole!'

'1928 - Stunn Brothers.'

'Pardon?'

'Electric fencing. First patented by the Stunn Brothers. Patent disputed by Dr Furbitz who claimed to be the original inventor. Hence the origin of the expression: 'I've been Stunned.'

'Thank you. That's all very interesting. Now let's just watch this jump, shall we?'

Hop-Pole jogged up, bent his pole to the mark and swung clear.

He made it look easy.

It was only a jump of three foot four, but even so.

'So he can jump. And he's no fool, this Hop-Pole.'

As he landed, cheering broke out throughout the stadium. Cheering and laughter, and pointing at the failed contestants.

'Ah that's not so nice,' said the Commentator.

'No, no,' said the Archivist. 'Funny though. I mean I can see why they're laughing. Fancy reaching the final with a jump of three-foot four!'

'So Britain's Harry Hop-Pole is through to the final. Join us next week to see how he gets on!'

Up in the loneliness of a small glass box, someone was unwrapping a round chocolate biscuit.

*

That night in the *Dog and Bucket* there were scenes of wild celebration. On the huge TV screen they played and replayed the epic contest.

Each time Harry walked over to the height-official laughter broke out.

'Here it comes, now! Here it comes, now! This is the bit where he tells him!'

'Wait, wait for it.'

'3 foot 4! Wha! Ha! Ha!'

And pints were raised and drunk in his honour.

Hop-Pole Mania

The next morning the papers were full of it. The country had found a new sporting hero.

'Unstoppable Hop-Pole' they called him.

'Hop-Pole Confounds!'

And in one paper, simply: *'Nice Won Harry!'*

But Harry knew none of these things as he and Scabbit tramped down the well-worn stairs and through the front door on the way to the café. It was a route they had taken many times before - down the hill, past the church, past the hedge where it all began.

'I'm going to go and get a paper,' said Scabbit. 'You go ahead - I'll see you in there.'

Harry shrugged, and went into the café.

The waiter came over with the menus.

Harry glanced back at the man at the next table. He was eating pasta-letters, guiding the letters about the plate with his fork, and muttering to himself.

'What's that he's eating over there?' asked Harry.

'Oh that's today's Special,' said the waiter. *'Alphabetti spaghetti - Tasty pasta letters in real tomato sauce.'* That's what is says on the tins anyway. It's for kids really. Helps them with their spelling while they eat. You don't want that do you?'

'No, I'll just have a bacon sandwich, please.'

'B-A-C-O-N,' said the waiter. 'See - I had mine this morning!'

Harry looked back at the man who was eating the pasta. He was wearing a denim jacket with the sleeves cut off and had tattoos down his arms - there was at least one dragon in there, it's coils twining and intertwining, its scales blue and a vivid, sickly-looking yellow.

'Ere' this is no good!' he said and flung down his fork. 'Not enough E's .'

'Alright, alright,' said the waiter. 'I'll go and have a look out the back - see what we've got left.' He gave Harry a despairing glance and headed for the swing doors.

'Can't even write my own name!' The big man stared morosely down at his plate.

'What's your name?' asked Harry.

'Ed.'*

*F.E. - This is none other than Ed of The Mean Riders - or to give them their full title: 'The Mean Riders Motor Cycle Club' - their adventures are chronicled elsewhere: 'The Mean Riders Ride!' 'Chrome is where the heart is.' etc.

Flagg is their undisputed leader (nicknamed Black Flagg on account of the fact that he never wears any other colour) the other members include Swordfish and Ed Rider. Swordfish is so-nicknamed because he has a tatoo of a swordfish on his right upper-arm, which he had done in Brighton at the tender age of fifteen. ' - I was going to get a shrimp - glad I didn't now.'
Ed, of course, went for the Dragon - a far nobler, prouder beast (than a shrimp). Not so good in a cocktail, though.

Anyway, I think perhaps we have dallied here long enough.

Scabbit came in with the papers. He had four of them tucked under his arm, and another sticking out of the pocket of his coat.

He looked furtively around him, then came over and sat down opposite Harry.

He leant over the table and looked him in the eyes.

'You're in 'em. You're in all of them!'

'What?'

And he was.

Pictures of him jumping. About to jump. And sitting out the back eating oranges.

'Where did they come from?'

Scabbit shrugged, and shook his head.

The waiter came over and put a plate down in front of him.

'What's this?' he asked looking down at the letters in their vivid red sauce.

'Sorry, wrong table!' and he whipped the plate away and put it down in front of the big man, who leant over it contentedly.

'You know what this means, don't you?'

'Yes!!!' said a voice from the next table, and a fist punched the air.

Nothing will ever be the same

People he'd scarcely known at school were suddenly eager to be interviewed and share long-forgotten memories of those far-off days.

'He was a great jumper even then,' said 'Old School Friend,' Danny Bickles. 'In fact I have to say he was the best jumper I ever met. Lovely lad, too. Lovely lad.'

They even managed to track down the old lady who'd been cleaning the hospital steps - the one who had held him in her arms all those years ago. Her name was Madge, she was 85 and was living in Broadstairs, Kent. 'He had a lovely little face,' she said. 'Not all squashed up like some of them. He was so quick, you see. I said to his mother, I said: 'He's a quick one there,' or 'You've got a quick one there,' or something.'

'Thank you, Madge,' said the interviewer.

*

It was the same everywhere. Even in the café. When he went up to pay at the till, Old Nick the proprietor just smiled.

'That one's on the house.'

'What?'

'You're famous son.'

And so he was. In fact the whole nation had suddenly become obsessed with the sport overnight. Sports shops redecorated their window displays and began to sell fine quality pole-vaulting poles, and every child wanted one. Cheaper versions were also available and the cries: 'Poles! Poles! Get your poles here!' were frequently heard on market-stalls where only a few days previously the same gruff-faced vendors had been mumbling half-heartedly about carrots and onions, and wilted spinach.

The same was evident in the media where TV schedules were hurriedly rearranged and experts were brought in to sit in comfy chairs and discuss: *'The Physics of Pole-Vaulting,' 'The Psychology of Pole-Vaulting'* and even to explain the more unsavoury aspects of this long-neglected sport in: *'An in-depth look at Pole-Tampering'*.

Pole-Tampering

'Well this evening we're very fortunate to have with us Sir Bernard Mikalis of the Pole Vault Council.'

A robust elderly gentleman with a sunburned face and large side-whiskers glared unsmiling at the camera.

'Sir Bernard?'

The elderly man tapped the earpiece he had been given and listened intently.

'WELL THIS EVENING…'

Sir Bernard jumped in his chair.

'Perhaps you could explain to us, Sir Bernard. What exactly is meant by the term: 'Pole-tampering.'

'Yes, well,' he wiped the side of his nose. 'Well basically, there are two types of pole-tampering.

One is where you tamper with your own pole - '

'And just to clarify. For our viewers. What would be the purpose of that?'

'Well to jump higher of course, there'd be no bloody point otherwise would there? I'm sure your viewers understood that already.'

'Well… perhaps,' said the interviewer, doubtfully. 'And the other kind? Tell us about the other kind.'

'The other kind of pole-tampering, and this is potentially more serious, which is why we are trying to stamp it out, and nip it in the bud so to speak, the other is when you, or someone on your team, tampers with someone else's pole.'

'Oooh that's not fair at all! Is it?'

'No it isn't.'

'Most unsporting! Have there been many cases of this?'

'Rumours, rumours… Always rumours.'

'Erm, right.'

'But we take all such rumours *very* seriously indeed,' and he brought his fist down on the table beside him with unexpected violence. The glass of water with which he had been provided jolted, and water slopped over the side.

'Well that was very interesting. Thank you for that Saint Bernard, I mean Sir Bernard,' he coughed. 'That was Sir Bernard Mikalis of the sport's governing body,' he sighed, and grinned inanely at the camera.

'Well that's all for tonight, but don't forget to join us for the event they're already calling...

The Final

The stadium was filling up fast and the touts were doing brisk business outside.

'Op-Pole tickets! Get yer Op-Pole tickets here. Buy any spares!'

'It's not right,' said Griffin. 'People making money out of an event like this. Bloody crooks. Should be ashamed of themselves!'

'Op-Pole tickets! Get yer Op-Pole tickets here,' said the tout. 'I'll buy any spares, Gents!'

'No you won't, sonny!' said Griffin, and he snatched at the wad of tickets the tout had ill advisedly wafted in his face.

'Hey! What do you think you're doing? I paid good money for those!'

'Yeah, well I'm taking them off you - that's what I'm doing,' said Griffin

'Don't bend them. Please don't bend them!' the tout whined

piteously. I can't sell them if you've bent them!'

'You ain't going to sell'em, sonny,' said Griffin, ' - 'cause you ain't having them back!'

'Three cheers for the honest gentleman!' cried a passer-by, wearing a Hop-Pole baseball cap. 'About time someone stood up to these crooks. These bullies!' he said shaking an arthritic fist at the tout. 'Hip-hip Hooray! Hip-hip Hooray!' Just then a battery of photographers appeared (three rows of them, one behind the other). 'Front Rank - Shoot!' There was a blinding flare of magnesium and the tinkling sound of spent flashbulbs.

'No pictures!' barked Griffin, blinking. He made a grab for the nearest photo-journalist, but 'didn't get a proper good grip on him,' as he admitted afterwards.

It was all very confusing. But finally they were through the gates. There was a palpable air of anticipation. Banners waving, a few mistimed firecrackers - either short-fuses or let off by over-excited spectators, and still people streamed in through the turnstiles.

'We're in F stand Upper T,' said Griffin looking down at his ticket.

'Upperty?' asked Jaundice.

'Mind you,' said Griffin. 'We *could* sit in any of these,' and he fanned out the tickets he'd snatched from the tout, with the understated dexterity of an expert card-cheat. He looked down at them with a poker face. Although his eyebrows did surge upwards when he found one ticket with a large crown printed on it, and read: *'Royal Box'*, but then he smiled to himself. 'These are fakes,' he said, happily. 'Fancy that! Our boy's so popular even the touts can't get tickets! Ha!' and with a heightened jauntiness of step he jostled his way to F stand Upper T.

Popular was the word. At that very moment a coach pulled up. A placard obscuring most of the windscreen proclaimed the arrival of: *Harry's Grannies*.

'What on earth?' An official in a bright-yellow coat stepped forward with his hand up.

The exasperated driver wound down his window and stuck his head out into the beautiful quiet fresh air.

'Never mind that, mate. Where can I drop this lot off?'

'Can't get in here without a ticket!' said the official.

'They've got tickets - God knows how.'

'We did a fund-raising knit-a-thon for a local charity and kept the proceeds!' said 'the inimitable' Granny Simms. 'Anyway, you can't teach us to suck eggs!'

'Look - if I were you…' said the yellow-coated official.

'Helloe Officer!'

'Hello officer! Officer!'

'I see what you mean,' he said. 'Look, tell you what, why don't you just unload them over there. I'll whistle for assistance.'

'I wouldn't do that - that'll only antagonise them.'

'Oooh, look! He's getting his whistle out!'

'Come along now ladies.'

'Oh we're coming alright! Just you open the door and see!'

The doors opened and they all tumbled out, and pushed and shoved their way through the turnstiles.

'You look like you need a drink, mate,' said the official.

The driver nodded. He put his elbows on the wheel and leant forward, resting his face in his hands.

'I've got to take them back, and all,' he said, and with shaking hands he lit a cigarette. 'Gave up last week,' he said.

'Smoking?'

'No, driving. They got me out of retirement: 'For just one more job.' Knew I shouldn't have taken it.'

Back in the arena

There were a few 'entertainments' laid on before the main event. The 100m sprint, the last lap of the marathon, the egg and spoon, and a few others, but no one took much interest in these and munched their way stolidly through crisps and sandwiches, and supped illicit cans of Eastern European lager which had somehow found their way into the stadium. Meanwhile down in the centre of the arena, a few tiny figures, made smaller by distance, stepped up on to boxes of different heights, and were given medals on long ribbons while the band negotiated a couple of unfamiliar national anthems. 'Phew,' said the conductor and got down off his own podium, after a verse or perhaps two, of: *The People's Independence Song from the Uncertain Federation of Neighbouring Parthian Hill Tribes.*

'Damn funny tune if you ask me,' said the conductor, scratching his back with the baton. 'All that stopping and starting. Gives you arm-ache. Glad that's over with.'

But then the screaming began and ticker tape showered down from the stands. A lone figure had wandered out on to the arena with his hands in his pockets.

'Harry Hop-Pole. Wearing his trademark red baseball cap, and the glasses he needs to see with,' as the Commentator informed viewers who could not be there in person.

'It's Harry Hop-Pole!' yelled a million and a half previously indifferent spectators.

'It's Our Harry!'

The grandmothers were crying and waving their handkerchiefs.

'We love you Harry!'

' - come all the way from Cleethorpes!'

Harry smiled and blinked, the sunlight catching his glasses as he turned to look round at the massed stands of waving figures. He waved back, which brought another upsurge of emotion: 'Oh look he's waving! He's waving at me!' 'Me too!' 'Oohhhh!'

Then he turned and went back into the tunnel.

Meanwhile out in the arena the jumping had begun.

'TOM-MAZ JINK-SKI!'

'The Great Russian' pounded down the track. His first jump was only 5 metres 70. A mere loosener. He jumped, landed, and got to his feet without fuss. Some members of the crowd stopped munching and applauded politely. Tommaz nodded, then walked back to the starting mark. The bar was raised, the tablets were held up: '5 metres 85' and he was off again.

But this time he clipped the bar on his way over, and the unfeeling white bar fell from its supports. 'Oh,' said the Commentator sympathetically. 'Hard luck.'

He tried again. And failed again.

The Great Russian sat on the blue bed, his weight making quite a dip in the mattress, looking down at his great feet. They had carried him many miles, these feet, all the way from a small mining town on the outskirts of Irkutsk (with temperatures reaching 110 degrees in the summer and plummeting to -40 below in the winter. Irkutsk.) But the journey was over now. He picked up his pole and walked solemnly over to where the journalists and photographers were gathered.

'Goodbye, my friends,' he said sorrowfully and with great dignity. 'It has been nice to know you.'

The Dreaded Uprights
(through which we all must pass.)

But before he could say more, two dark-coated figures intercepted him and led him away towards a darkened tunnel. He stopped in the doorway and waved back. Then he turned and was gone.

'I'll miss old Tommaz,' said the Commentator.

'Yes, he was an enigmatic character in many ways, and I never really understood him,' said the Archivist. 'But he was a great jumper in his day.'

'He certainly was. And I don't think he'll ever be forgotten. Oh, who's this now?'

'JA-AKE C-RANE-BILT!'

'Oh look, here comes Cranebilt!' observed the Commentator.

And out he came to a somewhat mixed reception.

'Oh isn't he just... gorgeous!'

'Get on with it yer big ponce!'

And he did.

It was classic Cranebilt - the smooth approach, the dip of the pole, the bend and the flight through the air. Cranebilt was over and clear. He stood up and kissed his pole. And asked for the bar to be raised.

'Oh look at that!' shouted Griffin. 'Kissing a *bloody* pole! What's the matter wiv im?'

Meanwhile, up in their cosy box with its bird's eye view of proceedings, the men behind the microphones were feeling peckish. It was time for a little snack.

'Very nice these little cakes. Would you like one?' said the Commentator.

'Phumpf-ah- fphumfa,' mumbled the Archivist.

'Ah, I see - you've already helped yourself. I wonder who made them?'

There was a pause while the Archivist swallowed. 'Perhaps it says on the tin. No, wait a minute, there's a note in the bottom. Ah yes, here we are: 'These cakes were made by Sister Ignatius Saul - by the labour of her own two hands."

'Isn't that nice! Well thank you very much Sister Saul, that's very kind of you!'

'Yes, very kind.'

'What a wonderful open-handed gesture,' said the Commentator. 'I think that's what's so nice about this Hop-Pole Summer - as it's being called - it really has brought the whole country together in a spirit of kindness, and generosity.'

'Yes, and then she says: 'Please can I have my tin back - a good tin is hard to find."

'Mmmm. Very wise words there, from Sister Saul. Well here comes Cranebilt again now - and if he gets this it'll be yet another world record!'

Again it was an impressive jump. The same smooth approach etc. the flight through the air etc. etc. All was perfect until he smacked into the crossbar, which caught him somewhere behind the left ear.

'Ooofffff,' said the Commentator. 'That looked rather painful! I wouldn't mind betting he felt that.'

He had. Cranebilt sat on the edge of the bed, his feet resting on the ground, his pole in his lap. He seemed to be slightly stunned.

For a moment so were the spectators.

But not for long.

Howls of derision, punctuated by groans of sympathy, and the odd sniff into a little white handkerchief.

Cranebilt had failed.

He tried twice more. And though he came close, oh so very close. He failed. For the first time in his career, Jake Cranebilt had reached his limit.

Cranebilt picked up his pole and walked away. Accompanied by his trainer with a towel over his shoulder.

It was a sad way for a great champion to go.

'That is a sad way for a great champion to go,' said the Commentator.

Throughout the proceedings, Scabbit had been standing on the edge of the track, his hands in the pockets of his long black coat.

When Cranebilt hit the bar, Scabbit stroked his stubbled

chin, the beginnings of a smile glinting in his eyes. 'Come on Harry, my boy,' he said quietly to himself, 'our time has come!' He turned away from the baying crowd, from the noise and excitement of the arena, and began walking up the tunnel.

Harry was out the back eating (more) oranges. He looked up as Scabbit ducked under the lintel.

'Come on Harry, time to jump,' he said.

'Alright,' said Harry. 'Let's go,' and picking up his pole, he walked down the long darkened tunnel and out into the glare of the arena.

The crowd went wild. They were ecstatic! Screaming his name and waving handkerchiefs, and banners, and little flags. Small children and babes in arms were held up to catch a glimpse of a thin, blurred figure with a long pole, (assuming they had the faintest idea where they were supposed to be looking).

'HA-RRY HOP-POLE!' said the Announcer's voice over the loudspeaker. (Not that anyone needed to be told.)

'Come on Opper's!' called a brickie from Bermondsey.

But even his voice, like many others, was drowned to all but those nearest him, such was the cacophony of the moment.

'Good luck, Harry,' said Scabbit.

'Thanks,' said Harry, and walked on alone.

'Here he comes now,' said the Commentator in a hushed, reverential voice. 'Harry Hop-Pole. The hopes of the nation resting upon his slender shoulders. On his slender legs and shoulders.'

But the crowd was in no doubt.

'You can do it Hopper's!'

'One more jump and he's yours!'

'You've got him Hopper's!'

'Of course the important thing now,' said the Commentator, 'is for Hop-Pole not to lose the initiative.'

'What do you mean exactly?' asked the Archivist.

'CAM ON 'OPPER'S!

CAM ON 'OPPER'S MY SON!'

'Well,' said the Commentator, 'he's still got to actually jump over the *bar* - otherwise all this is meaningless,' and he gestured around him at the massed-crowds, the ticker tape, the advertising hoardings, the howling and waving, and a million private acts of public madness.

'Ah, yes, that's true,' said the Archivist, nodding in agreement.

'Very true.'

Harry walked over to the height-official and leant over to speak to the little man.

'Alright?' said Harry.

'I'm... I'm F-fine,' nodded the official, warily.

All around them the crowd was in uproar - a continual rolling wave of sound.

'So what's it to be?' asked the man with the tablets.

'I think we'll go for... 7.50,' said Harry.

'7.50??? But… but…'

'Alright, then 7.75. But I don't think I can manage much more than that.'

'But the upright's only go up to 7.70!'

'Oh I see, fair enough. Well let's make it 7.70 then.'

He turned and walked back to his mark.

The little man poked away at his tablets. There seemed to be some problem getting them to work. Meanwhile he spoke into a little mouthpiece.

The bar was raised.

And raised.

The tablets were held aloft: '7.70'

Even the Announcer picked up his binoculars to make sure his eyes were not deceiving him. Then, he flicked the switch to 'Transmit' and leant forward.

'SEVEN METRES SE-VEN-TYYYY!'

'7 metres 70!' said the Archivist. 'But…' and he looked helplessly at the piles of soon to be obsolete texts about his feet.

Down in the arena, stood a lone figure with a pole.

On televisions sets all round the world, the same images were being seen. In the middle of the night in some places. An insomniac in Melbourne yawned and switched channels.

Five miles away, on the top floors of a tower block, people with their windows open could hear the sounds of distant cheering.

Then suddenly all went silent.

Hop-Pole raised his English Yew Pole and tapped it a couple of times on the ground, adjusting his grip slightly around the shaft. Then he picked it up and ran.

Like a cheetah.

A cheetah with a pole.

All around him there was screaming, and cheering, and the waving of flags.

But he saw none of these things. His mind was a crystalline tunnel, and at the end of that tunnel, the focus of his entire being - was a window of light above the bar, through which he was about to pass into immortality.

Ignoring the cheers and the screaming and the shrill, hand-clasped declarations of love, he ran, braced himself upon the pole, the stout English Yew pole, which bowed under his weight, before catapulting him up and away.

Everything seemed to go into slow motion then, and for a few precious moments he seemed to hang in the air above the bar, before turning and allowing himself to fall backwards.

No two people who were there that day saw quite the same thing. To some it was as if he was a diver doing a backflip off a boat to dive into the sea. Or a drunk falling backwards off a bar stool - but however he'd learned the technique - and at a later date there was to be some speculation - all agreed that he seemed to hang there in the air for a while before coming back down to earth. Earth, in this case, being the blue bed, which gave under his weight, and then sprang back into place, to cacophonous cheering.

'One small step for mankind!' shouted the Commentator. 'But a great leap for Harry Hop-Pole!'

One of the grandmothers had fainted and had to be brought round with smelling-salts, the half-hearted wafting of a black-lace fan, and a kick in the ribs from one black-booted grandmother who had been a matron in a field-hospital before her retirement 38 years previously, and was in no mood for messing around.

'Oi! Get up you old sausage!'

'Granny Simms!' said a by-standing grandmother.

'Does'em good, trust me.

Or I'll do it again.'

'Well that's all we have time for!' said the Commentator.

But it wasn't, quite.

Epilogue / Man in a coat

A man in a long black coat was seen shouldering his way up through the stands.

'Hey mind out!'

'Watch where you're putting your blinking feet mister!'

But the blinking feet went onwards and upwards. To the small glass box high above the arena.

To those down below there seemed to be some kind of struggle up in the little glass box. But perhaps it was just one man giving up his seat to another. Then a voice came over the loudspeaker system - slightly nervous at first, but growing in strength and confidence:

'When time has passed, and time has gone, and all we've loved has come and gone...'

The man in Melbourne switched channels again, then yawned and went to bed.

The End.

You have been watching:

(All characters will be caught in likely poses and will smile pleasantly as the camera lingers upon them.)

Mickey Jakes - the landlord of the *Dog and Bucket* standing beneath his newly painted sign. Ah, the ready host! Just opening up for the day.

Mandy Jakes - wife of landlord Jakes. A kindly, vivacious woman with an excruciating laugh. Loves flower-arranging. Particularly hydrangeas. Hello Mandy!

Allsop the barman - barman *and* cellarman of the *Dog and Bucket* Public House. Can be 'a bit of a tyrant' on occasion. Here he is polishing his beloved tap handles.

Eric Babbings - a burglar. A small man in a flat cap gives us a nod. Former bantam-weight boxing champion, known for his straight left and short-temper, carries this black canvas tool bag everywhere.

Charles Jaundice - Plannings Officer of the local council. Has been described as 'a weasely ferret' by one of the other characters. Here we find him signing letters with his very fine tortoiseshell fountain pen.

Chindlin Bob - the last pole-carver in England. A master of his chosen craft. There he is look, hard at work gleefully treddling his pole lathe.

Constable John Phlebbs - a policeman. Not known for his mental agility. (His thought processes have been likened to 'rainwater percolating through peat'.) That's his helmet on the table in front of him. He is frowning. A sure sign that he is thinking!

Jim Griffin - an underworld boss. Head of the Syndicate - an organisation that meets secretly in the upstairs room of the *Dog and Bucket* from which he looks out over the rooftops of *'Our Town'*.

Henderson - *'The Big Fat Piano-Player'* - another underworld boss. (Note: Henderson's 'patch' is the other side of the river from Griffin's - the river forming a natural boundary between the two.)

Sister Ignatius Saul - in her rather austere black bonnet. Sister is a well-intentioned collector of funds for good causes. She makes wonderful cakes too - like the one she is holding.

The Vicar of Fillingbourne Stoutly - *'Isiah! I-siah! Isiah!'*
At this point his head bowed and the vicar fell asleep, his

spectacles at the end of his nose, his hands on the notes in his lap.

Jake Cranebilt - An American pole-vaulter. A truly outstanding athlete. Fine set of teeth.

Tommaz Jinkski - A Russian pole-vaulter. Also known as *'The Great Russian'* or *'Jumping Jinkski'*. A popular figure whose eyes have seen sad things. Here come his attendants in their dark coats. Goodbye Tommaz.

Jacques Flèche - an underrated French pole-vaulter. Known for his occasional bursts of 'flair-vaulting' in which he approaches the sublime. An erratic performer. Walking off dragging his pole behind him. Oh, didn't even say: *'Au revoir.'*

And lastly, here he is:

The Professor - What? You haven't met the Professor yet? Well here he is in his black gown inspecting his collection of moths. There they all are in their little glass frames. Motionless. Drugged beyond stupor. *'Professor?'* Oh, he can't hear us. Lost in his own little world. Or perhaps it is us. Perhaps *we* are fading, drifting away…

A short history of pole-vaulting

> **- a lecture by The Professor**

The Professor raps smartly upon the sloping wood of the lectern and we are away...

'Well now well now *hugh hugh hum.*'

He fiddles with his notes and adjusts his spectacles.

A rather hesitant start this from the Professor. The air in the auditorium is one of rapt, of intense... someone coughs. It is the Professor, himself - ah, he is off: 'I am sure you have all heard of the great deeds of our wonderful athlete Harold Hop-Pole. And since I know how popular he is with all you young people, I thought I would devote this evening's lecture... to pole-vaulting.

You are probably wondering what an old fool like me knows about a sport like that?'

They certainly were.

'Well historians believe that the first pole-vaulters were in fact shepherds who would cross rivers by leaning on a pole and jumping across to the far bank. The first pole would therefore have been the shepherd's crook.

The shepherd's crook,' he says again.

An assistant steps out of the wings and hands the Professor a shepherd's crook.

'Sorry - almost missed my cue there.'

The assistant disappears behind the scenes. (Until called upon at some future time.)

The Professor traces the curve of the hook with a boney finger. 'As you can see, the shepherd's crook has a pronounced 'hook' here at the end of it. This is known as: *'The hook at the end of the crook.'* Now this was originally designed for recapturing or 'hooking' a wayward or recalcitrant member of the flock.'

(At this point the Professor springs forward and playfully hooks a boy in the front row.)

'Like that you see.

Ha! Got him!'

A smattering of good-natured chuckling from the audience.

Red-faced boy struggles but is well and truly hooked. The Professor kindly disentangles him. Boy rubs back of neck. The Professor smiles.

'Of course what we shall never know - is whether the first shepherd to cross a river in this way was simply fooling around, or whether he was in fact a diligent shepherd who was crossing the river in the course of his work - a stray sheep perhaps.'

He feints with the crook again. Red-faced boy sways back out of reach.

'Ha - not so easy see. Surprise is everything!'

More good-natured chuckling. What an eccentric old cove our Professor is!

The Professor pauses for thought. Still clutching the crook. (Boy in front row still scowling.)

The Professor resumes: 'What is known is that the first centres of pole-vaulting were the flat lands - Holland, Belgium and our very own Norfolk fens, although curiously not in the Somerset Levels where pole-vaulting never really took off and traditional crafts such as basket-weaving have prevailed.

'However!'

(The Professor raps the crook on the ground, startling his audience.)

'How-*ever* - what we can be *more* certain of is what happened *after* that first momentous river crossing.'

The Professor snorts and shakes his head woefully.

'All too soon, shepherds everywhere were abandoning their flocks! Their competitive spirit had been aroused - one shepherd competing against another - a sad state of affairs - sheep wandering alone and without guidance, lambs bleating pitifully, the tang of the ragged wolf upon the air...'

And then all a-tumble the words came to him, and the auditorium was filled with the flat-croaking music of his vision as his words leapt and soared, and all who were there (except for one in the front row) agreed it was simply the finest thing since old Arbuthnaught had told the stirring tale of his adventures among the Azbecs and even that had its lowpoints - the recipes and such. But the Professor just swept them all up along with him and before they knew it he was saying:

'Thank you and goodnight.'

And suddenly the Professor is descending the hallowed steps amid tumultuous applause. He smiles and nods smugly by way of acknowledgement.

A few questions for our students:

1. So who did invent the sponge-bag? Was it Cleopatra?

2. Why is the salmon thought to be so wise?

3. So how come he gets caught?

4. Who was born in Irkutsk?

5. What was the weather like there?

6. Here are the Contents of Babbings' Tool Kit - can you spot the odd one out?

One trusty old wrench, one pair of wire-cutters, one pair of heavy-duty bolt-cutters, crowbar, picks and feelers, glass cutter, knife for picking out putty, one expandable drawstring bag. 'And me torch - a *Pharos Lightbeam* - they don't make'em like that anymore.' A half-eaten pork pie.

7. What is the moral of this story?

(*That old chestnut - F.E.*)

8. What is the Piano-Player's real name?

A selection of out-takes

How our beer comes to us - by Allsop the barman

Bobbin and Dobbin the ancient shire horses what drag the big heavy cart reluctantly through the throbbing (froo the frobbin) streets of our town lugging them great big old wooden barrels (casks) the beer all slopping about - like a big foamy wave crashing against the inside of the lid in the darkness as Bobbin and Dobbin go plodding on and on etc. etc.

*

where once the sweet crowds sang

The scene in the arena after the event - the empty silent stands echoing with cheering, the paper cups and ketchup-smeared chip-plates underfoot, the silent stars above, and the worm who came up fearing rain.

A short extract from the next Wispy Gorman story:
Chef of Distinction!

The Swallow

The sun had scarcely risen when Dick Scabbit drew back the curtains.

'Good morning world!' he said.

The sky was pale-pink over the rooftops, there was dew on the grass and the air was still. Scabbit slid up the window and took a deep breath of the morning freshness.

And there in the cool morning air - was a swallow. The first swallow of the summer! Scabbit watched entranced as it looped and fluttered, dipped, slicing through the air and flittered its wings. Scabbit, who loved all forms of wildlife, took this as a sign, an omen. This was a sign of new beginnings. A summer full of promise lay ahead. A summer of sunlight and laughter. A summer of dreams and new beginnings. Of barbecue smoke and raised glasses and happy customers. He could see it all in his mind's eye.

The swallow had flown all the way from Africa to tell him this.

And now, having attracted his attention, it was tired. It perched on a length of guttering on the house opposite, its wings drooping, its head on one side.

What has the swallow really come to tell Scabbit?

Find out in the next instalment! - *Bet you can't wait - F.E.*

Wispy Gorman - a few autobiographical details.

Birth / The Early Years - this period is dealt with in more detail in the highly entertaining: *'Wispy Gorman - the autobiography'*. Was nicknamed 'Wispy' on account of his being a thin, undernourished child. Even the loyal family doctor once commented: 'My God! Look at those ribs - don't they feed you at home?' This upset the young Gorman who was already developing into a withdrawn, sensitive child. Mrs Gorman wasn't too happy about it either. Next - *The World of Work* - Wispy took a job as a clerk and toiled for a few months in a dingy office beneath a railway bridge. The bridge had a leak and after heavy rain, the steady: *drip! drip! drip!* was quite hypnotic. Wispy frequently fell asleep, especially in the afternoons. Invited to leave, Wispy accepted and went to live in Spain, the land of the siesta. These were happy, carefree years and Wispy began writing poetry. *'Oh Luna! Luna!'* etc. After a few years he returned with an old, beech-framed trunk bulging with poems. He lived in an attic in Lambeth enduring all kinds of hardship and poverty in pursuit of his art. It is this period of 13 years which inspired and informed *The Wispy Gorman Stories.*

The Wispy Gorman Stories:

Harry Hop-Pole

Chef of Distinction!

The Ray of Truth

Dick Scabbit and the Reindeer

The Finger of Destiny

The End of the World.

acorn book company

is an independent
publisher of small, high quality editions.

For more information
please visit us at:
www.acornbook.co.uk

FOR SALE

One big floppy blue bed.
Forget King size - this is Emperor size!
Would suit fat emperor (plus retinue).